# "We're too close to the past, too close to Jonathan."

Kathryn paused. "I don't think it would ever help either of us to talk."

Adrian put out his hand. "It's worse keeping things in." The touch of his hand on her bare skin was treacherous.

"I'm sure Jonathan lied to you about me," she said huskily. "If I only knew what he said."

"You were the only person in the world he ever really cared about," he told her. "Some of his letters were wonderfully tender."

Kate's full lips trembled. "What right had you to get inside our marriage?"

"Jonathan wanted help, Kathryn. And it's important you accept help now. You're entitled to it, God knows."

"I won't listen to this." She started up quickly and felt his hand grip her shoulder. "Don't touch me," she warned, and her mind filled with panic.

**MARGARET WAY** takes great pleasure in her work and works hard at her pleasure. She enjoys tearing off to the beach with her family on weekends, loves haunting galleries and auctions and is completely given over to French champagne "for every possible joyous occasion." Her home, perched high on a hill overlooking Brisbane, Australia, is her haven. She started writing when her son was a baby, and now she finds there is no better way to spend her time.

## Books by Margaret Way

### HARLEQUIN ROMANCE

2490—HOME TO MORNING STAR
2537—SPELLBOUND
2539—THE SILVER VEIL
2556—HUNTER'S MOON
2591—THE GIRL AT COBALT CREEK
2609—HOUSE OF MEMORIES
2634—ALMOST A STRANGER
2639—NO ALTERNATIVE
2658—A PLACE CALLED RAMBULARA
2700—FALLEN IDOL
2724—EAGLE'S RIDGE

### HARLEQUIN PRESENTS

270—RING OF FIRE
549—BROKEN RHAPSODY

# The Tiger's Cage

## Margaret Way

# Harlequin Books

**TORONTO • NEW YORK • LONDON**
**AMSTERDAM • PARIS • SYDNEY • HAMBURG**
**STOCKHOLM • ATHENS • TOKYO • MILAN**

Original hardcover edition published in 1986
by Mills & Boon Limited

ISBN 0-373-02784-2

Harlequin Romance first edition August 1986

# CHAPTER ONE

'Isn't it marvellous, you can earn so much money without doing anything strenuous?' Pam said.

'Marvellous,' Kate agreed calmly. 'More coffee?'

'Lovely.' Pam pushed her cup forward. 'I love our little talks.'

'I'll have to cut it short today, Pam,' Kate apologised. 'My solicitor wants to speak to me.'

'Your solicitor! How grand.' Pam waved a sarcastic hand. 'I remember when you couldn't even afford to talk of one.'

'So do I. *Nouveau riche.*' Kate was thinking it was sad that her small successes had kindled resentments in her old friend, 'A dollop of cream?'

'You do spoil me.' Pam sighed voluptuously. 'How's the little man?'

'Much better!' Kate said gratefully. 'At least his allergy hasn't stopped him from growing. He's going to be tall.'

'Like Jonathan.' Pam's pretty mouth tightened. It was five years since Kate's husband had careened off the road in a drunken haze, and ended his life in a ditch.

'Like Jonathan certainly and like me, too. I'm taller than average. You only remember the painful things about Jonathan. I remember the good things.'

'Good things, rubbish!' Pam stirred her coffee furiously. 'He gave you a rotten time.'

'And himself a worse time. He loved me in his way.'

'I suppose he did,' Pam considered when she could vividly recall Jonathan's passion for his wife. Indeed she had been deeply envious of it. Pam loved Kate, but their friendship had been complicated by Pam's jealous nature. Kate was the talented one, the kind one, the girl with the cloud of raven hair, gardenia skin and great Delft-blue eyes. Pam was unpredictable, volatile, sharp-tongued yet fiercely loyal. She made people nervous when Kate serenely ignored all her sarcasms.

'You could have done far better than Joanathan,' she said abruptly, and for the umpteenth time. 'He was absurdly handsome, but so shallow and selfish.'

'He's dead, Pam,' Kate said without emotion, turning to blink away the swift, involuntary glitter of tears.

'You would have divorced him anyway,' Pam started up again. 'What would your grannie have thought about that? Her beautiful Kathryn divorced! The unimaginable sin! He was really weird, Jonathan. He was mad about you, yet he was always trying to bring you down. He even made a pass at me.'

Kate bore this calmly. It was Pam's way of denying Jonathan's complete indifference to her. 'Jonathan had a painful childhood,' she pointed out sombrely. 'A stable childhood is central to everything surely? Jonathan's was sad.'

'But were his stories true?' Pam looked sceptical.

'In essence I would think so.' Kate's brilliant eyes were sad and remote. 'It only took a brief moment of conversation with his parents—his mother rather—to realise not to measure up would be the cardinal sin.'

'And all that money!' Pam threw up her hands. 'Jonathan who never had a cracker, actually came from a rich family. I can't get over it. I'll never get over it. He left you without a cent. Worse, up to your eyes in debt.'

'I managed.'

'Because your friends stuck by you,' Pam said impatiently. 'And because you have this fantastic talent for drawing. I never thought when you were doodling all over our school exercise books that you were going to be able to make yourself rich.'

'Hardly rich, Pammy.' Kate looked back at her.

'Anyway richer than me. Adam did it for you. Good old Adam! Seen him lately?'

'Well, yes, the other afternoon. I wish I could love him. I do love him. But——'

'You don't want to go to bed with him,' Pam said bluntly. 'They all love you. I wonder what it is?'

It was said with so much grievance that Kate burst out laughing. 'To tell you the truth I think it's because they know I would refuse if they asked me.'

'Maybe!' Pam shrugged. 'At least you *had* a sex life. Married at eighteen, playing the loyal little wife to a perfect cuckoo. You've had four guys breathing down your neck since and what do you do? Sit at home with Cam. It bothers me.'

'Don't let it,' Kate smiled.

'You're bright. You're beautiful. You're too beautiful. I'm not game to bring a guy of mine here.'

'You do though.'

'Because you're so compulsively nice and friendly and you're such a great cook. I'm twenty-four, Katie. I want to settle down, not drift aimlessly through my days. You're the one with all the would-be lovers and you're not even interested.'

'Oh, I'm interested all right,' Kate said wryly. 'It's just I'm not interested in experimentation. If I can't care, a sexual relationship wouldn't feel good. Besides, I have Cam.'

'You were brought up too strictly,' Pam said gruffly. 'Abandon yourself, like me.'

'Try playing hard to get with the next guy you meet.'

'It would never work.'

'Try it.'

'I'm not controlled enough.'

'Stop underestimating yourself,' Kate said briskly. 'I'm not sure why exactly, but men always hanker after the woman they can't get. If I were you I'd try spurning a few advances and then maybe a real relationship might take hold. I thought Greg was genuine, but you're so uptight, you scared him off.'

'I know, I know.' Pam shook her tawny head. 'It still hurts about Greg.'

'Ring him.' Kate leaned over and gripped her friend's hand. 'Tell him you valued his friendship, and miss it. Promise him you won't drag him into bed.'

'Do you think it would work?'

'No one is going to hang you if you try.'

'Smartass.'

'I really care about you, Pammy. Go back to being yourself. Relax. It will all happen.'

They stayed silent a few moments holding hands, then Pam sighed deeply. 'You married your first man. You must regret it. The family refused to have anything to do with you.'

'They didn't really, Pam.' Kate stood up. 'I didn't want anything to do with them.'

'You'd have liked them to accept you all the same. You didn't tell them you were pregnant.'

A breeze blew up, scattering the sheets on the drawing board and Kate clutched after them. 'I was too proud, right?'

'Real proud. You're the first person I've ever met who's *real* proud.'

'I had the idea that they would think I wanted money.'

'And didn't you?' Pam gave a brittle laugh. 'You nearly starved.'

'No, I didn't.'

'You had friends.'

'Don't think I'll forget how good you were to me,

Pammy.' Pam in fact was a much better friend in adversity than good fortune. 'Besides I had to look after myself for Cam's sake.'

'You had a lot of guts,' Pam cast her eyes down.

'I didn't even see it that way, there was so much support. I'll be grateful to Adam until my dying day. It was a miracle that he thought of showing my sketch books to Saunders.'

'God bless him!' Pam cheered ironically. 'There's nothing Adam ever liked better than playing your knight in shining armour. It's a wonder he didn't blow his brains out when you married Jonathan.'

'For God's sake!' Kate put a hand to her suddenly aching temple.

'I'm serious, sweetie. Adam has been your adoring slave since Grade Five. Personally I like your little boy character much better than the girl. She's just that wee bit saccharine.'

'Well, the great thing is she sells.' Kate passed lightly over the criticism. She realised Pam was going through a period of lowered self-esteem, when it nearly killed her to say nice things. On the other hand her own career as a freelance illustrator was soaring, making enormous changes in her life. Nowadays she could afford household help in the form of Dora, who was always on hand to look after Cam. Such good fortune occasionally put Pam in a bad mood, plus the fact that Kate had her studio at home thus reinforcing Pam's opinion that Kate wasn't really working at all. How could it be difficult, drawing one hundred little flower faces while carrying on a conversation?

Pam sat on, automatically leaving Kate with no time at all to change. Usually she put on a dress for visiting Mr James, but now she only had twenty minutes to get into the city and park. The parking was the worst bit. She detested the huge, high-rise parking lots, being mildly claustrophobic.

It took two minutes for Kate to brush out her heavy mane of hair so it was a mass of deep, springing waves; a few seconds to retouch her mouth and another to catch up her shoulder bag of softest Italian leather. How she loved leather, the smell and the feel of it. Mr James might be astonished by her boots and skintight stretch jeans, but her silk blouse in a glorious shade of wine silk did marvellous things for her colouring and it was classic in design.

'What's it all about?' Kate asked her reflected image. In her girlish young dreams, she had never expected to be a widow at twenty-four with a small son to rear. Only her own talent had allowed her to rise above despair. A sense of futility came on her now and then, though. She wanted a man to love her. Really love her, for herself, the person. Jonathan's perspective had been almost exclusively sexual. He had disassociated himself from her developing personality with its underlying strength. They had interacted badly.

Just as it had been Adam who put her on the road to success, so it was Adam who sent her to McCawley, James & Associates to help her unravel the legal tangles Jonathan had left her in. Kate was deeply grateful for the fatherly way Mr James had advised her. Indeed she still called in occasionally to say hello, and the firm had done the conveyancing on the charming little cottage that was her first real home.

Kate had been orphaned very early in life and reared by the best of grandmothers. Her grandmother had died in Kate's seventeenth year and her memory was sacred to her granddaughter, indeed Kate had called her own little son Cameron, her grandmother's maiden name. It didn't seem strange to her that she had always been so often alone, though her heart had often ached for family. Probably with Gran to advise her, she would never have married Jonathan. Gran would have seen through Jonathan at once. The eighteen year old Kate had been so very trusting and vulnerable. A young girl on her own. Jonathan, six years her senior had dominated her easily. For a while.

'Kate, my dear!' Ronald James looked up at his secretary showed Kate into his office. He stood up and came around the desk, holding out his hand.

'How are you, Mr James?' Kate responded with pleasure.

'Delighted to see you.' The twinkling grey eyes alighted on her outfit, the very slender young body and the long, long legs. 'You look very . . . trendy.'

She smiled at him with her enormous blue eyes. 'My apologies for the jeans, but it was a job to get away.'

'Would you like a cup of tea?'

'I'd love it!' Kate slipped into the chair he indicated. 'I had to sprint the last block.'

'In those boots?'

'We women are used to them.'

'Crazy.' Ronald James, if he had been asked did he miss not having a daughter, would have said yes.

'You were very mysterious over the 'phone,' Kate faced him over the cup of tea.

'It was difficult to explain to you then,' the elderly solicitor said, almost anxiously. 'I have a feeling you might not want to hear my news.'

Kate felt her heart constrict. 'Is it anything to do with Jonathan or his family?'

'How intuitive you are, Kate.'

'It's the Celt in me.'

'Ah, yes,' Mr James felt himself drowning in those brilliant blue eyes. 'As you know we set up your business in your maiden name, O'Connell, and you're listed in the 'phone book under that name which made it a little harder for your . . . in-laws to find you.'

'You mean they found out about Cam?' Kate snorted with the light of battle in her eyes.

'The most extraordinary thing happened,' Mr James told her. 'It was one of your cards. Some member of the family was struck by the resemblance between the face in the illustration and the young Jonathan Dowling.'

'It's Cam,' Kate declared with sudden passion.

'Cameron strongly resembles his father. You've told me that yourself, Kathryn.'

'Yes.' Kate dipped her head as though in exhaustion. 'So now they want to see him; interfere in my life. Perhaps even make an attempt to run it.'

'They are Cam's grandparents, Kate,' Mr James pointed very gently.

'They showed no kindness to *me*,' Kate countered. 'And I'm Cam's mother, for all they couldn't bear to accept me as Jonathan's wife.'

'Thank God you've been such a brave, resourceful woman,' Mr James blinked. 'Though how they failed you I'll never know. You would please any parent.'

'I didn't please them. Mrs Dowling was very cold and remote. Mr Dowling appeared to be a sick man.

'Well they owe your son something,' Mr James said.

'Cam and I are getting along perfectly well as we are,' Kate said indignantly.

'Don't misunderstand me, Kate. I think they only want to see you and to try and make amends. People are never themselves, at funerals.'

'It seemed to me they harboured an enormous grudge.' Kate looked back through the years.

'He was their only son.'

'He was just one big disappointment to them, Jonathan said.' Kate breathed a deep sigh. 'Jonathan seldom spoke about his parents, but I wasn't surprised to find them the way they were. Jonathan never once returned home after he left. Understandably he found it bitter to be regarded as a failure. He told me the day he met me that his family no longer existed for him. I was very sad for him and very thankful he had me to turn to. Jonathan took all the comfort I could give.' There was no need to say that he gave none.

'Knowing you, Kate, I would have thought you'd try to mend the breach.'

'I wanted to find out what it was all about,' Kate murmured, her slender hands tightening, 'but Jonathan used to become very angry whenever I suggested he re-establish contact with his parents. I thought everyone wanted family, but Jonathan didn't. Our arguments became so increasingly bitter after a while it was safer to leave well alone. If Jonathan didn't try to see his parents, they didn't try to see him.'

'As you say, sad.' There was the shimmer of tears in Kate's blue eyes and Mr James looked away.

'Heartbreaking.' Kate dashed an impatient hand across her eyes. 'I always thought Jonathan's emotional problems stemmed from his unhappy childhood and adolescence. He was rather desperate about being loved, yet at the same time he would go out of his way to be ... unlovable. It caused us both distress. I suppose it follows that if you're not loved as a child, you become very insecure. Apparently, Jonathan had a cousin who completely overshadowed him while he was growing up, to the point where he felt his father was always comparing him unfavourably with the other boy. Adrian, that was his name. I remember it very well. Adrian always figured in Jonathan's life. It seemed he was brilliant, but a very unfeeling person.'

'He had enough feeling to wish to trace you.'

'Why, how very peculiar!' Kate went quite pale. 'Are you trying to tell me it was this Adrian who started the trace on me?'

'If Adrian is Adrian Pender, and he must be. I understand he's been in England for some time. Brilliant fellow—a Q.C. One of the youngest ever to take silk. Top legal family, of course. A man like that would be extremely observant. He followed the whole thing up. One could conclude that he thought the family had treated you very unfairly, as in my view they have. You are rearing a son . . .'

'It's Cam they're after,' Kate interjected. 'I'm quite certain this Adrian Pender doesn't care about me. Jonathan couldn't speak of him without emotion. One could call theirs a strange love-hate relationship. Apparently the Dowlings and the Penders attach a great deal of importance to demonstrating their superiority. They must be very clever and competitive, but Jonathan couldn't compete against this Adrian. His jealousy was massive.'

'Which would certainly colour the impressions he handed on.'

'Probably,' Kate nodded, 'but I'm prepared to bet Adrian Pender is not hero material, no matter how heroic his achievements. He must have hurt Jonathan endlessly, perhaps even driven him away. Families like that can be problematic. Jonathan looked to his parents and to his cousin, for approval, but he never got it. It's as simple as that. It was the same with me. In fact I was astonished people like that existed. My grandmother's whole existence was the joy of love and sharing. She had the most selfless, pure spirit. She wouldn't have understood Mrs Dowling either.'

'My dear, I've upset you. You've gone very white.'

'Perhaps I understand their wanting to see their grandson, but only a fool would walk willingly into the tiger's cage.'

'It mightn't be like that at all, Kate.'

'I could lose my freedom. These people are in a position of wealth and power and Adrian Pender is a man of brains and ambition. You can be certain he's acting for the family and in their interests. They can hardly want me. It's Cam they're after.'

The solicitor shook his head. 'Did they never discuss your future?'

'It was a terrible funeral,' Kate said bleakly. 'I wasn't their concern at all. The bond with me was broken when Jonathan was killed.'

'But your looks, your manner, everything about you is so positively charming,' Mr James protested.

'You're extremely kind to me,' Kate said. 'But that's how it happened. Everyone needed to blame someone and I was chosen. It was very wounding, but I had my pride. Had Mrs Dowling been a different sort of woman, I might have told her I was pregnant, but it was only too clear she wanted to abandon me.'

'I don't pretend to understand any part of it,' Ronald James sighed. 'How could anyone be indifferent to a grieving young widow?'

Kate threw up her raven head. 'We were all suffering. They knew nothing about me and how could they? Jonathan wanted no part of his family when I worry all the time about Cam. What would happen to him if anything happened to me? We only have one another. He has no real grandparents to love and spoil him, or rather he had no grandparents.'

'They've surfaced now, Kate,' Ronald James said gently.

'All because of Adrian Pender. Don't you find that astonishing?'

'Can't you bring yourself to meet them?'

'What good would it do?'

'They could help you. They could help young Cameron. I know you're making your own way, and I'm very happy to see you so successful, but the Dowlings have always had what you'll have to fight for. They have an established position in society, as well as a great deal of money. They could give Cam every chance.'

'They couldn't do it for their only son.'

'You've only heard Jonathan's side of the story.'

Kate bit her lip in distress. 'I'm afraid that's true.'

'Don't you think it takes a little time to get at the truth?' Ronald James asked earnestly. I know you're very loyal, but didn't you tell me—didn't you *have* to tell me—that your Jonathan had problems and that you had begged him many times to seek professional advice? On the surface Mrs Dowling may have seemed an unreachable woman, but she may have been experiencing acute suffering. Perhaps even guilt. Could there be a more powerful love-bond than mother–son? Maybe Jonathan drained her supply of love and hope just as he was draining yours?'

'You're suggesting it was Jonathan's fault?'

'I don't know the answer to that, Kate, but you could be in the position to find out.'

'Instinctively I'm dead against it,' Kate's emotions were in a whirl. 'Had the Dowlings learned I was childless I'm sure I wouldn't be here now. Their sole interest is in their grandson.'

Mr James nodded his silver head, not denying the truth of her words.

'What exactly is it they want me to do?'

'Meet them,' the solicitor replied swiftly. 'I guess what they really want is to make amends, and meet the little person who so clearly has the family face.'

Kate was so perturbed that the first person she called was Adam. He soothed and comforted her, he even fathered her, but they had never made love, much as Kate knew Adam wanted to. It wa sad and ironic that Adam was everything Jonathan had never been, but one couldn't call up physical passion at will. Kate loved and trusted Adam as a dear friend, but the idea of sleeping with him was made impossible by her total lack of desire. She didn't understand why it was so— Adam was an attractive, heterosexual male and, more importantly, he was deeply attracted to Kate, but somehow she could only see him as a friend; someone she really appreciated without feeling in the least romantic about. Adam had asked her to marry him—not lately—but despite Kate's refusal, phrased as gently as she knew how, they were still comfortable with each other.

Now they sat together at the lunch-table and Adam was showing no surprise at the news Kate unfolded.

'It was bound to happen, Katie,' he finally told her, his mouth twisting in a wry smile. 'With some people it's the grandchildren they love most.'

Kate's breath fluttered. 'I feel they might want to take Cam over, not share him.'

'Well of course they may very well be that kind of people. I've heard of Pender.' Adam picked up his wine glass and downed every drop. 'He's the brilliant son of a famous father, grandfather, indeed great-grandfather, if you want to go further back. The Pender are one of our top legal families. Surely you've heard of Sir Leon Pender? He's always heading some commission or other.'

'That Pender?' Kate experienced an unexpected shock. 'Are you sure?'

Adam, much upset, managed a nonchalant shrug. 'You must have missed an article in the *Bulletin* some months back. We were given a whole tour of the family, including a lovely picture of father and son against a wall of weighty legal tomes. A very handsome, superior pair. Don't you just *hate* the legal world? Self-satisfied elitists. Why ever would Pender have interfered in this matter?'

'Partly because Jonathan was his cousin and partly because the Dowlings must want their grandson.'

'If I had a grandson I would want him very much.'

'I don't think they want me, though,' Kate pressed her white fingers to her temple. 'And I've only just figured out that if these Penders are so clever and powerful, they might like to prove I'm not the best person to raise my son.'

'Nonsense, darling,' Adam said sharply. Usually he was careful not to use too many endearments with Kate, but the sick expression her face had shocked that one out of him. 'I'm sure they only want to invite you to their home so they can get to know you and their grandson. You're an excellent mother and you're making it in a highly competitive world.'

'Being such rotten snobs, wouldn't they think illustrating cards was just as trivial as it could be?'

'I wish *I* could do it,' Adam's lean, bony face lightened with humour. 'You make more money than I do as a bank accountant . . .'

'I know they would think it a very lightweight profession.'

'Who cares? Most people would admire a clever woman.'

'Clever?' Kate held up her hands. 'I have a certain talent.'

'Most people have little talent at all,' Adam said sincerely. 'You're beautiful, Kate.'

Kate smiled. 'You mean what else does a woman need?'

'Now, now, don't start that feminist stuff. I know your views about women's lib and allowing women full development, but gosh, could there be anything better for us males than looking at a pretty woman? They lighten the day, every day and don't you know it. Beauty is a billion-dollar business and when you come to think about it, beauty is rare. Perhaps even rarer than talent. The fact of the matter is, men pursue beauty, whereas women pursue security. The way you look, I predict this Pender character could even fall in love with you.'

'Adam!' Kate stared at him in astonishment.

'A face like yours alters lives.'

'It certainly hasn't helped make things easier for me,' Kate said. 'Jonathan had no great use for my mind.'

'Jonathan didn't have much time. What he felt for you physically, was central to everything.'

'In short, woman is a sex symbol.'

'Largely, yes. Isn't it desire that brings man and woman together? Desire brought Jonathan into your life just as the lack of it is keeping me out. We don't fall in love because someone is good or decent. Of course it's better if they are, but falling in love is outside of the rational. It's chemical. A beautiful woman has a lot of power. *You* have a lot of power. I even used to feel sorry for Jonathan at times. No, dear, let me speak——' Adam leaned over and grasped Kate's hand. 'You were the best wife in the world and Jonathan did every thing in his power to destroy you, but all along he knew what you knew. You no longer loved him . . . in fact, you had never loved him. You were in love with an ideal, with having someone of your very own. Before you were married, no one could have been more engaging than Jonathan. I used to look at him very carefully to be sure he was real, but underneath the boyish charm he was deadly. Almost from the day you were married, he never missed an opportunity to try and hurt you. Perhaps your triumph, who knows, maybe it was your mistake, was to drape over his faults with unexpected skill. You made it nearly impossible for Jonathan to expose the cheapness of his character. He couldn't even shape an insult that you couldn't manage to turn aside. Jonathan judged you to be a born victim. You were very young and you were all alone. Those of us that knew you, realised that you had a lot of strength, but Jonathan hated your strength. It was, to him, perhaps your least desirable characteristic. It was devastating

for him to think he had married a very malleable
young girl, who was totally dependent on him, only
to find he had married a woman. A *real* woman.
Look at the way you've come through your ordeal.
You're beautiful and brave, Katie. That's why I love
you.'

'How good you are to me, Adam,' Kate said
gratefully. 'I would never have really managed without
your help.'

'My dear, you would,' Adam shook his head, and a
muscle flexed in his cheek. 'Would to God you would
marry me, though.'

'Please, dear.' Kate looked deeply troubled.

'It's a queer business isn't it, this love? I've always
thought of you as my girl, yet you married a
stranger—a man of an unpredictable and menacing
temperament. It was inevitable he should die
violently. The miracle was he didn't take you along
with him. Sometimes I think that was the way he
wanted it. If he couldn't have you, no one else could.
It seems melodramatic, but that's the way of it with
some men—with some women too. Look at the crimes
of passion. I don't know which was the worse—
Jonathan's marrying you or your marrying him.'

'You mean it might all have ended differently?'

'He was wildly in love with you, but you were no
good for him.'

'Do you think I haven't thought that?' Kate cried.
'It tortures me that I hastened Jonathan's descent. He
wanted a woman he could dominate and make suffer,
but I refused to accept either. I threatened him with
divorce, but he merely laughed at me and told me I
could never go so far, but in his heart he knew I was
desperately serious. I had to act for my son, for his
future. One does what one must.'

'Yes.' Adam lowered his eyes from Kate's pale,
distressed face. 'I suppose if you even allowed Cam's

grandparents to see him you would be acting far more generously than they deserve.'

'So what is it to be?' Kate asked anxiously. 'It's something of a burden to me to know my son would be quite alone in the world should anything happen to me. I'm out in my car every day—I could be involved in an accident. There's so much we can't foresee!'

'Then why don't you allow them the opportunity for reconciliation?' Adam's hazel eyes searched Kate's with deep understanding. 'If they're just too terrible, move out.'

Kate gave a wry laugh. 'Jonathan inherited his strangeness from someone. I'm fearful of bringing Cam into contact with any unpleasantness. He's such a happy little boy. All he knows is love and good-hearted people.

'Jonathan might well have been a one-off. A black sheep. Some mothers do 'ave 'em, as they say. In any case, Katey, whatever it's like, you can handle it. You've been tested. You know your own resourcefulness and inner strength.'

'I guess I do,' Kate relaxed slightly. 'And I suppose I have the psychological edge too. They rejected me when I might have needed them. I don't need them now and while I'm alive, neither does my son. My God, though,' she cried emotionally, 'isn't that it? Cam needs his grandparents. Why aren't they the right kind?'

'You only met them once, Kate, and in the most terrible circumstances.'

'Yes.' Kate's blue eyes shadowed to inky darkness. 'It was a ghastly time, yet Mrs Dowling did an awfully good job of freezing me out. Don't you hate really cold people? That's never going to happen to my Cam.'

'My darling I hope not!' Adam groaned. 'Why are we getting so morbid? Your in-laws have asked you and Cam to stay with them for a short whole, most people would understand and be sympathetic towards the request.'

'Except I had the feeling Jonathan's mother was an odd woman and I'm good at assessing people.'

'That's you,' Adam reasoned. 'She just saw a beautiful young face instead of the person you are. She may have weighed you up and judged you quite wrongly. She may have had reasons for thinking her son had been unhappy. She may have transferred *her* guilt feelings to you, who knows? That was in the past, maybe now she feels the need to repair it. Perhaps you and she will never have a close relationship, given such a bad start, but I'm certain there's not a grandparent on earth who could fail to love Cam. He's a grand little chap and a truly caring little person. He takes his looks from his father, but I'm beginning to see a lot of you in him. I am certain his grandparents will love him dearly, and I'm sure they'll want to do something positive for him, like ensuring he has a bright future. You're a young woman, Kate, and beautiful too. One of these days you'll remarry. Your path hasn't been easy, you've had to struggle too hard. You'll want a time to devote yourself to enjoying life. There has been a lot of worry so far—nurturing a baby when other girls your age were out enjoying themselves with a string of boyfriends.'

'I established early in life that I wanted a family,' Kate said.

'I know. You've often spoken of it,' Adam said. 'Your relationship with your grandmother was beautiful, I can only pray it's going to be the same way for Cam and his grandmother.'

# CHAPTER TWO

It was a long time since Kate had felt so nervy and apprehensive. She stood in the lounge of a busy airport watching a uniformed chauffeur striding towards her, with a purposeful look on his rather heavy-set face.

'Mrs Dowling?'

'Yes.' She inclined her head firmly, tightening her grip on Cam's small hand. 'You're my father-in-law's chauffeur?'

'Yes, madam. Ralph Goodwin is my name. I'm a little late—forgive me, but the traffic was very slow.'

'No matter,' Kate's expression eased slightly. 'My son was enjoying all the activity. He has never been in a plane before.'

'Enjoy it, did you?' the chauffeur asked the little boy, his dark eyes narrowing on the entrancing little face.

'It was super and so quick!' Cam looked up at his mother and smiled. 'I think I'll be a pilot when I grow up.'

'Well it makes a change from a policeman.'

'Is this your luggage, Madam?'

'Yes.' Kate signified the pieces and the chauffeur loaded them on a trolley and began wheeling it towards the door.

'I can do that,' Cam suggested excitedly.

'Oh, no you don't,' Kate said.

At length they were settled in the back seat of a very elegant dark blue Rolls and Cam, who was already something of a car enthusiast, began a very thorough inspection of the interior appointments. 'This is a nice car, Mummy.'

'Isn't it?'

'Nicer than ours,' Cam commented, smoothing his hands delightedly over the fine Connolly leather. 'Are we going straight to my grandpa's house?'

'Yes, darling.' She put her hand over his and squeezed it gently. Why have I brought you here? she thought. To lose you? For an instant she was shot through with panic. Cam was everything in the world to her, indeed she was awed by her love for him, which set his well-being far above her own. She could only pray she had made the right decision for she had the certain feeling that once they were in her life the Dowlings would be very difficult to get out.

The journey proceeded regally with Cam chattering excitedly and Kate hoped fervently that the car trip wouldn't bring on one of his attacks. Cam was allergic to so many things, dust, pollen and certain foods; indeed there was rarely a month that Kate was free from anxiety. She, who was blessed with a near perfect respiratory system, had borne a child who suffered agonies of sneezing and wheezing. Kate bent down and kissed Cam on his round forehead and as she did so her inner courage flared. His big, grey luminous eyes assured her how much he loved her. Nothing on earth could part them.

'We've arrived, Madam,' the chauffeur announced as they turned into the driveway of a house that was hidden completely from the street.

'Gosh, it's *big*!' Cam looked up at his mother, round-eyed. 'I might even be able to get a pony.'

An elderly man in working clothes appeared from the right, reaching out a hand to one of the massive stone pillars that supported the black wrought iron gates and as he did so they swung open.

'Magic!' Cam breathed.

Great shade trees lined the curving drive and back

from them spread the gardens ablaze with spring flowers.

'How beautiful!' Cam clapped his hands. His delight in nature was inherited from his mother, and now he responded to the glories of a large garden. Kate had made the cottage very attractive, with lots of indoor plants and hanging baskets, but a narrow little garden strip could hardly compete with what looked to be three acres of Eden. There were great drifts of azaleas, stately magnolias, rhododendrons rising like great green walls and spectacular mass plantings of anemones sheltering under the trees; daffodils, jonquils, narcissus planted in curving drifts and colonies of daisies that trailed down the sunny slopes. No one who had such a garden could be all bad, Kate thought. How could one love nature with a passion without also having a deep knowledge of human love? Then again, they could have a marvellous gardener.

'I never thought it would be like this,' Cam said. 'Did you, Mummy?'

How could she not smile at him, and encourage him to reach out at this new experience with open hands? Cam knew nothing of her conflicts, the hard times. He would never know if she had her way. She had explained to him that Daddy's parents, *his* grandparents, were longing to meet him and because she wasn't as busy as usual—which wasn't true—she had decided to accept their very kind invitation to visit them.

'I expect they'll love me!' Cam had announced, love being all he had ever known.

'Of course they will, darling. Little grandchildren are very special people.'

The house was a picturesque stone Tudor, enormous by Kate's standards, with wide swathes of leaded glass windows and the walls of the west wing almost completely covered in ivy. It was very grand, very elegant, but not, Kate thought with sudden foreboding, particularly welcoming. It was almost as though the house wasn't in ultimate harmony with the sun filled beauty of the garden—which was decidedly odd. Kate wasn't altogether pleased with her Celtic intuitions.

'Where is everyone?' Cam demanded. 'Why aren't they coming down the stairs?'

'Steady, dear.' Kate felt the need to restrain him. 'Your grandparents will be waiting inside.' It seemed rather restrained of them, Kate thought, marvelling at how differently her own Gran would have acted. Gran would be rushing at them with open arms. The great pity was that she could not. It would have been the greatest joy to Gran to hold Kate's child, now only the Dowlings were offering.

The chauffeur held the door and Cam tumbled out. Apart from his eyes, he was his father's child, but his enthusiastic abandon was all Kate's; the natural assumption that he was loved and wanted. That had been Kate when she married. Love freely offered, returned with a twist of sadism.

'Do wait, darling,' Kate called, leaving Goodwin to bring the luggage, and hurrying after her excited child. Cam had been brought up to respect property, but there was no telling what he might knock over in his haste. He was so energetic, far more than an orderly child. 'Cam, don't run away,' Kate begged.

'I won't, Mummy.' He paused sweetly and obediently. 'It's so wonderful here!' He threw up his hands at the blue-violet jacarandas abloom on all sides, then clapped them delightedly together. Kate had bought him a new outfit with new shoes and socks and, for all his allergies, he looked a beautifully made, blessedly healthy child. His mobile little face was rosy and dark silky curls nestled around his head like curving petals. Few women could look at him without an outflow of maternal love. He was an adorable little boy. Kate reached him and held him, but after a moment mother and child became aware a woman was approaching through the gothic archway.

'Nanna?' Cam asked, looking up into Kate's face.

'Yes, darling,' Kate responded with more ease than she felt. 'Let's go and say hello.' This wouldn't be fun for either woman, but at least Cam was relaxed and happy.

'Nanna!' Cam began to wave, and as a result Marcia Dowling came out of a slight trance and held out her arms warmly.

'Cameron, dearest boy!'

She was rewarded as Cam ran to her eagerly, only too ready to give and receive love and attention.

'Cameron,' his grandmother bent to him, 'this is so beautiful. I can't believe it! You're really here.'

'And Mummy!' Cam looked from one to the other encouragingly.

'Kathryn, how very good of you to come to us,' Marcia acknowledged, looking very formal, but still sincere. 'We are so grateful.'

'I just adore your house, Nanna!' Cam announced, his face flushed and smiling.

'Your house, dearest boy, when the time comes.'

It's started already, Kate thought protectively. No matter how hard she tried, she could never hope to match Cam's grandparents in material possessions. Being a privileged child had not helped Jonathan, so she wasn't altogether sure it was a good thing offering Cam too much, too soon.

'Do please come in,' Marcia caught Cam's hand with a deft movement. 'I feel so excited, you have no idea!' Yet her whole image was one of svelte, slightly daunting elegance. She wore a classic, blue silk shirtdress with a single string of large, lustrous pearls and the abundant fair hair Kate remembered so well, was arranged in an updated chignon. Kate thought her very striking.

'Grandfather had an appointment this morning but he hopes to meet his little grandson at lunch.'

'And Mummy!' Cam told his grandmother sunnily, as if to remind her.

'And Mummy,' Marcia echoed playfully and ruffled Cam's silky curls. 'My darling I would have known you anywhere. By the way, Kathryn,' the reflective mood snapped, 'we're giving a little dinner party for you this evening. Just family and a few close friends.'

'Why, thank you, Marcia,' Kate responded pleasantly, feeling a little lurch of apprehension. Would she be up to a party? Adrian Pender would surely be there. One would be automatically compelled to become a High Court judge with a name like that. She knew already they would be antagonists, even though hostility was foreign to her nature. For a young woman who had suffered a good deal in her short married life, Kate was remarkably free of bitterness if not all the hang-ups.

Cam, hand in hand with his grandmother, was moving into the grand entrance hall, utterly enchanted. 'Oh, there's a man in a tin suit!' he cried in wonderment.

'That's a very old suit of armour, dearest,' Marcia told him with pride. 'We have so many wonderful things to show you, and all the time in the world.'

Kate had told them in her letter that she and Cam would be staying a *month*.

Cam, tired out with all the excitements, was already fast asleep when Kate dressed for dinner. The crucial meeting had gone beautifully and it comforted Kate a great deal to know the old, ugly wounds could be allowed to heal. Cam had gone off to bed yawning widely and Charles Dowling, sick man though he appeared to be, had not been able to contain his pride and joy in his new-found grandson. Cam had accomplished in seconds what no one else had been able to do. Kate would always cherish the expression on Charles Dowling's worn, handsome face as Cam lifted his arms spontaneously and wound them around his grandfather's neck. 'See how happy I am, Grandpa!'

Could anyone bring people together as swiftly and sweetly as a child? Both women shared Charles Dowling's intense pleasure and Marcia, who had remained frozen at her son's funeral, wept openly. 'Would to God Jonathan had been like that!' she sighed deeply.

Kate was confounded. Jonathan had painted a very bitter picture of his mother and a mother's love, now she was receiving indicators from the other side.

Her bedroom was quite beautiful. The whole of one wall was a big, alcoved window below which ran a seat piled up with exquisitely trimmed cushions. The view was directly out over the rose gardens, and their luscious scent permanently pervaded the air. There was a huge carved and painted canopied bed with filmy drapes and a *chaise-longue* upholstered in the same glowing floral chintz as some of the window seat's cushions. A painting of pink camellias in a turquoise *cloisonné* bowl hung over the white marble fireplace and an exquisite Chinese rug echoing the rich pinks covered a large area of the parquet floor. Pink camellias, too, were arranged in a silver bowl on the small circular table near the window, and Kate grew calmer and more at home in such a graceful setting.

'A beautiful room for a beautiful young woman,' Charles Dowling had told her. 'I want you to be happy here, Kathryn.'

The grimness of the past seemed to be forgotten. It was all one could wish for.

Her make-up done, Kate slipped into her dress. It was perfect for this kind of occasion, she thought gratefully, and she had been extremely fortunate to secure it at an end-of-season sale. Its colour was a glowing royal turquoise with silver beading at the throat and shoulders and at the centre front of the wide cinch belt and with it she wore the silver leaf earrings Adam had given her the last Christmas. Her evening shoes were silver and she had dressed her hair more elaborately than usual to make it stand up and away from her face and then cascade over her shoulders. She had always worn her curly hair full and flowing. She was tall and slim enough to carry it in such a style, and it disliked being tamed in any case.

'You'll do!' she told herself as she looked in the mirror for a final check. Nevertheless she felt a pull of nerves in the pit of her stomach. No matter the courtesy she had been shown, it was Cam they really wanted. Adrian Pender had not gone to such lengths just for her. But she could not think of that now. Life tended to follow a pattern. It had never been easy for her and it wasn't going to be easy now.

Her precious boy was fast asleep, lying on his side, one hand tucked beneath his cheek. Was his breathing a little raspy? Kate bent anxiously, as she did so often. She couldn't detect it now, but she would look in on him again.

'My dear, sweet little boy!' Recognising her gentle kiss, Cam smiled in his sleep.

Underneath Kate's habitual poise was a deep well of sadness. Cam had been deprived of a father. Jonathan had not wanted children. She had discovered that very early in their marriage, all the time expecting him to change, but his resistance had been rigid.

'I've no wish for children, Katie. All I want is you.' She had been astonished how charming he could be in certain moods, how forbidding other times when her heart contracted in alarm. Jonathan had done his best to break her.

Kate cast aside her unhappy thoughts and walked through her bedroom door to the long gallery. It was hung with paintings and she realised from the names they were very valuable. The most she had ever known was to be comfortable, yet Jonathan had grown up rich. It had not been a good thing.

Gracefully, Kate began to descend the stairs, her hand resting lightly on the gleaming bannister. The chandelier in the entrance hall was enormous, as it had to be to illuminate such a large area. Kate half veiled her eyes at its brilliant dazzle, stopping for a moment to absorb its magnificence. One couldn't beat a chandelier for sheer spectacle, though it would be a nightmare to clean.

When she looked down again, a tall, dark haired man came to the door of the drawing-room and it was as if all solid ground had fallen away from under her. She clutched at the bannister, her heart lurching so violently that, for a tenth of a second, she thought she might die.

*Jonathan.* She stood paralysed, her face betraying her intense shock. Nothing in this world or out of it could have rendered her so nerveless. The weakness was so powerful that though her lips were open, she couldn't make a sound.

'Kathryn?' He half turned abruptly, his eyes a brilliant diamond grey and through her sick miasma Kate detected answering shock waves. 'I regret. I've startled you.'

*You've startled me out of my mind.*

The pounding in her heart eased dramatically, though she felt cold and giddy, as light as air.

'My dear ...' He came up the stairs with long, urgent steps, grasping her arm, His voice was as anxious as the taut expression on his handsome face. 'I've shocked you. I'm so sorry.'

She appeared to flinch, though it was obvious she was desperately in need of his supporting arm.

'Sit down on the stairs for a minute.' He spoke calmly in the midst of the turmoil, using his strong lean body as a prop for hers with one arm encircling her back. 'Put your head down.'

Apparently she was unable to respond, for his hand came around her nape, applying just enough pressure to make her bend her head. The effect was extraordinary, holding her to earth. The whirling sensation went away and the blood began to course in her veins.

Presently he said, 'Feeling better?' He upturned her head, looking down into her ivory-pale face. Her dark hair was cascading back in inky contrast and her intensely blue eyes were of such a size they seemed to swallow up her face. 'I think you need a brandy,' he told her quietly, reaching out to push a long silken strand of hair from her cheek.

'I'm all right.' That was as far as she could get.

'You're not. I could lift you quite easily.' He rose and she gave a little stricken gasp.

'Please . . .'

'It's perfectly normal in these circumstances.'

She shook her head. 'I'll be all right in a moment. I think the earth moved for a time.'

'No one ever told you of the close family resemblance?' He sat down again beside her, fantastically handsome, like Jonathan, but with so much strength and high intelligence showing through. Jonathan had never aspired to such presence and authority. His voice had not been so assured and decisive. He was not Jonathan at all.

'You are quite frighteningly like him,' she said shakily. 'Then again, you're not at all like him. Just a cruel jest of the gods. You must have thought I'd gone quite mad.'

'Let me take you down to the library,' he urged gravely.

'It might be an idea. I can't keep sitting on the stairs.' She gave a choking little laugh and he helped her up, keeping an arm locked behind her. 'Jonathan told me a lot of things about you, Adrian, but not *that*.'

'Be quiet for a little while.' He was aware of the trembling right through her body.

'I should have known the first person I would meet would be you.'

He didn't respond, but led her into the restful quiet of the library, putting her into a deep velvet-upholstered winged back armchair. Her colour was returning, but it was obvious she was thoroughly off-balance.

'Come, drink this!' He put a brandy into her hand.

'I suppose I'll have to. One could scarcely drink it for pleasure.'

'Some do.' His smile in so grave a face was a startling revelation. Unhappily, Jonathan had never smiled like that.

The liquid rolled like fire down her throat and around her heart and she gave a little panting breath. 'It's wretchedly effective.'

'It is. You'll feel better in a moment.' He took the crystal brandy balloon she was offering like a child after medicine.

'I do.' Her mind and body were warming and she understood why the stimulant was necessary. She gave a little sigh and tipped her gleaming head back against the paisley velvet.

'You're very beautiful, Kathryn,' he told her, his eyes on her delicately boned face, the beautiful full mouth. 'I knew you must be.'

There was a curious sadness—or was it mockery?—in his tone and her eyes opened wide. 'Why is that?'

'Jonathan would never have married a woman who was not.'

'You must be a very romantic family.' She responded more bitterly than she intended, so a tense silence fell. Jonathan's passion for her had been physical, but the clamour in his blood had allowed for little tenderness. There had been no romance, indeed her marriage had been the bleakest period of her life.

'You've a little more colour in your cheeks now,' he remarked eventually, in a courteous but detached tone. 'I'm glad.'

'Shall we say the first stupendous shock is over.'

'The last thing in the world I wanted was to upset you.'

His gaze was so clear and direct that Kate had to lower her eyes. 'You make me feel so ...' she struggled helplessly.

'What?' He had been leaning against the carved mahogany antique desk, now he moved closer.

'Confused. Guilty.'

'Guilty? That's ridiculous.' There was almost a cut in the black velvet tone.

'Perhaps, inevitably, we make each other feel guilty,' she suggested, and a faint shimmer of tears overlaid the Delft blue of her eyes with silver.

'Kathryn, that's nonsense.' He rejected it out of hand. 'Don't you think you owe it to yourself—to me—to try to sift through the distortions to the truth?'

'Surely you're not saying Jonathan was a liar?' She didn't wish to recall that *she* had called Jonathan a liar often enough. Not that he often tried to keep his deceptions from her.

His mood, like hers, was becoming decidedly edgy. 'You understand perfectly well what I mean, Kathryn.'

'I understand, certainly, the relationship between you and Jonathan.'

'But surely not? You were never able to observe it.' The light from a tall, standard lamp emphasised the startling cool brilliance of his eyes. 'I hoped, Kathryn, we could lay down the overwhelming pity of the past. I grieved for my cousin.'

Something in his tone upset her dreadfully. 'And I did not?' Pain flowed in her. Dark memories. 'I can't bear this!' She swung her head so he couldn't see the expression in her eyes.

'Please—don't distress yourself.'

'It's impossible not to.' Her voice was shaken and hushed.

'You'll feel calmer soon. Let's talk about your work. I'm envious of your talent.'

'Surely you would despise anything so trivial?'

'On the contrary, I think you're very clever. You're just in a mood to set yourself against anything I say.'

She knew she was. 'I would expect a barrister to take that view.'

'It's such a beautiful night, Kathryn, so relax.' He walked to the window and drew the long heavy curtain aside. Outside the moon was making its majestic upward progress. 'Jonathan fell very deeply in love with you.'

'I thought he did.'

'Come here. The rose garden looks magical by moonlight.'

She swayed up and came to his side, hearing him give a faint sigh. 'He did, Kathryn. We always kept in touch.'

'No.' Her denial was shocked and fluttery. 'Jonathan told me he had finished with his family.'

'As small boys we were inseparable,' he said, as though he had barely heard her. 'I thought of Jonathan as a younger brother.'

'And you were the big brother he could never hope to match?'

He turned his handsome head abruptly, studying the challenge in her face. 'Isn't there enough alienation as there is?' he asked, his tone just severe enough to suppress her. 'For a long time no disaffection existed. There was never any thought of competition in my mind.'

'So when did things begin to change?'

'You've had a shock. I think you should go quietly.'

'As you say, Adrian.' She shrugged ironically.

He turned his head away and looked out over the garden and the masses of roses that were pale and delicate as carved ivory. 'I suppose we began to change at the usual age,' he said sombrely. 'When one passes from boyhood, finding one's adult identity is fraught with risks, as you already know.'

'Meaning I married too young?'

He put out his hand and tilted her chin so the moonlight gleamed on her face. 'Possibly you married someone who wasn't . . . right for you?'

'And Jonathan, your cousin.' The touch of his hand on her skin was filling her with alarm and despair. 'I thought the family had agreed it was Jonathan who had made the mistake.'

His hand dropped abruptly. 'Perhaps it was a mistake for Jonathan to get married at all. Or at least at that time.'

'Well, Adrian,' she said heatedly and moved away from him, 'marriage is a very private affair, as you may discover when you try it yourself.' Anger danced in her and a queet, unwelcome excitement.

'Anger has made you forget your shock,' he told her with a wry smile. 'Your eyes are like great sapphires filled with an unholy light.'

She swung around to stare at him. 'I know this might happen every time we meet.'

'So.' He continued to smile.

'Why did you bring me here?'

'Long after time.'

'Even if I have no place here?'

'Would you cut Cameron off from his family?'

She looked defensive and bit her lip. 'Cameron my dear Adrian, is my affair.'

'Of course.' Now his voice became cool and gentle. 'I'm looking forward to meeting him. Children bring such joy. My uncle looks a changed man already.'

'Yes.' She stood still staring sightlessly at a row of leather bound books tooled in gold. I'll remember this night all my life, she thought. The past and the present have come together. It was too much. *He* was too much.

Marcia came to the library door, looking from one to the other as she caught the strange urgency in the atmosphere. 'Oh . . . you've met one another?'

'Yes.' Adrian walked towards her, not bending to kiss her cheek as Kate expected, but taking Marcia's extended hand. 'I didn't even need to introduce myself.'

'How could you?' Marcia's voice dropped. 'I'm so glad you were able to come. We never seem to see you any more.'

'Sometimes my work cuts me off.'

'You're so ambitious, Adrian. Even for an already renowned family.'

It was said with a smile, but Kate considered it a barbed remark. She had expected Marcia to dote on Adrian, but her intuition told her there were negative undercurrents.

'How marvellous you look, Kathryn,' Marcia now said with open approval. 'Your dress is perfect. I remember the first time I saw you . . .'

'I've grown up a lot since then.'

'You have indeed. We're absolutely thrilled to have you here, and Cameron is the fulfilment of our hopes and dreams. By the way, my dear, what is his second name? Surely we can fit in a family name?'

'His second name is Jonathan, Marcia,' Kate told her.

'He should have been called after his grandfather,'

Marcia frowned. 'None of us can hide the fact my son
lacked his forebears' strength. But the ordeal is over.
Cameron is a fine boy—the good genes have taken care
of that.'

'Yes. He's a lot like my own family.'

Marcia looked surprised and started to speak, but
fortunately she was interrupted by the arrival of the
first of her guests.

'That was naughty, Kathrỹn,' Adrian drawled and
smiled at her. 'Marcia doesn't care for challenges of
any sort.'

'I hope that's not true, or we'll be frequently at
odds.'

The rest of the evening went well. Kate sat at
Charles' right hand while the conversation at the table
of sixteen flowed around her. Sir Leon Pender, whose
name came up frequently, was unable to attend, but
Adrian's mother was there.

Once again Kate saw the family face. Olivia Pender,
in claret silk, was a magnetically beautiful woman and
strangely she and Kate took to one another on sight.

'My dear, I have longed to have you in the family,'
she said. 'Already we owe you so much.' As she spoke
she looked at her brother, and her face was filled with
love and compassion. Charles Dowling, looking up,
bowed his head in their direction. Tonight, illness
seemed to be forgotten and his fine, worn face looked
lighter and younger.

Seated beside Adrian was Davina Adams who had
come along with her parents who were long-standing
friends of both families. Davina was a small, very
slender blonde, her upswept hair showing off her
delicate neck. Her champagne coloured dress had the
same sparkle as that wine and it was very obvious she was
intensely attracted to the man beside her. She had
greeted Kate with determined affability, though some of
her questions and remarks over the long, leisurely

dinner betrayed a faint sting. While several of the guests professed themselves familiar with Kate's work and charmed by it, Davina seemed disposed to poking fun at her. She herself had just been admitted to a firm of women lawyers which was enough to say that one could hardly expect her to be captivated by so slight a gift.

Once, when Adrian looked across the table to Kate, Davina didn't even try to hide her displeasure. There had been nothing in Adrian's expression to make her jealous, but Davina's bright, shrewd, green eyes made it quite clear to Kate that Adrian Pender had been claimed long ago.

Kate was deeply embarrassed. She had strong feelings about the man, but they were the wrong kind. It was unbelievable that Davina should act that way. Kate sighed deeply and resigned herself to the other woman's antagonism. It was a punishing thing in lots of ways to have out of the ordinary good looks, for other women were inclined to see competition where there was none.

Most of the guests had made their farewells when Cam looking flushed and distressed made his way into the library after checking the hall and the drawing-room.

'Why, darling, what's the matter?' Kate, who had been speaking to Olivia, sprang up at once and Cam ran right into her arms.

'I feel wheezy.'

'Oh, Cam!' She had known it in her bones.

Charles and Adrian stood up, staring almost raptly at mother and child, but Kate missed the shadow of grief that passed over their faces. Cameron may well have inherited many qualities from his mother, but everyone was familiar with the startling combination of black hair and grey eyes, the finely cut distinctive features. Everyone remembered Jonathan as a child and his son was his most perfect creation.

'Whatever is wrong with the boy?' Marcia asked anxiously. She went to Kate and attempted to take Cam from her arms.

'No!' Cam, experiencing difficulty with his breathing, held tighter to his mother.

'It's all right, Marcia,' Kate said soothingly. 'It was probably the plane trip. Cam is allergy prone.'

'Goodness!' Marcia's regal face looked dismayed. 'Is it emotional?'

'Not at all.' Kate clamped down on a little spurt of anger. Cam's wheezing breath was hot against her skin. The distress her little son suffered was through no fault of his own, or of hers.

Olivia came to them, bending gently to kiss Cam's flushed cheek. She did it so naturally that Cam lifted his head to first stare, then to smile at her. 'Who are you?'

'I'm your Aunt Olivia,' Lady Pender said. 'How lovely to meet you, Cameron. I would have known you for a Dowling in all the world!'

'You're pretty,' Cam smiled, then hung his head on his mother's shoulder.

'He'll outgrow these attacks, Kate,' Olivia offered comfort.

'Oh, I do hope so.' Kate flashed a glance around the room. 'Please excuse me, won't you?'

'Certainly, dear.' Marcia looked on, rather stern faced.

'Mummy!' Cam suddenly wailed.

'Ssshh, darling, sshh, my love.' Kate rubbed his back.

'Here, I'll carry him up for you.' Very gently, but firmly, Adrian prised the boy from his mother's arms and Cam offered no resistance, but closed his arms around this strange man's neck. 'Hello ...' He hesitated, confused by a feeling of familiarity.

'Hello, Cam,' Adrian returned warmly. 'If you move around on my neck, we can make this a game.'

Cam gurgled wheezily and complied, tightening his grip on Adrian's throat and all of a sudden Marcia's face began to pucker.

'Come up with us, Marcia,' Kate kindly urged, but a strange bitterness flashed into Marcia's eyes. 'I don't like to interfere, Kathryn, but you won't solve this problem babying Cameron.'

'Oh, Marcia, you don't know. I've had Cam to the top specialists. Even they don't have many answers.'

'You've seen them?' Marcia insisted.

'Marcia, dear, Kate has just said she has,' Charles intervened. 'Don't hold her up now. Cameron will be needing her.'

'Surely not with Adrian there,' Marcia returned amazingly.

'Oh, Marcia!' Lady Pender gave a low sigh and moved back.

Adrian was already at the top of the stairs and Kate caught a glimpse of Cam's large, bright eyes. They were full of acceptance and a curious serenity as though he revelled in this man's attention. And why not? Kate thought bleakly. Every little boy needed a father. She tried to obliterate her unhappy toughts. If Jonathan had truly loved her, he would have wanted their child.

When Adrian lowered Cameron on to his bed the little boy bounced upright. 'You'll have to give me my tablet, Mummy.'

'What does he take?' Adrian turned to Kate with a slight frown.

'Antihistamines and Ventolin. I don't feel guilty about giving it to him. He really needs it.'

'How could you think I'm questioning your actions, Kathryn? I only asked.'

'With a disgusted frown on your face.'

He shook his dark head. 'You're over-reacting, my dear.' He put his hand on Cam's shoulder and Cam looked up at him trustingly.

'Listen to my funny breathing, Adan.'

'Adrian,' Adrian smiled.

'Adan,' Cam repeated obediently.

Kate looked at them no longer, but went for the tablets. The one thing she had not anticipated was the sight of her adored little son snuggling comfortably against Adrian's shoulder. For so long now she had been filled with a deep mistrust of him. Not all of Jonathan's talk could have been lies.

Cam took his half tablet without fuss then lay back while the two adults on either side of the bed talked to him gently. Then, without warning his eyes shut and his heavy lashes swept his silken cheeks.

'There, he's asleep!' Adrian murmured with satisfaction. 'It's quite incredible how like Jonathan he is.'

'Or you,' Kate added bleakly, with a pang in her voice.

'Don't hate me, Kathryn.' He sat quietly, looking at her.

She was silent, twisting her wedding ring around her finger, as though it was cutting deeply into her flesh. 'I don't hate you. How could I? You're a stranger to me.'

He put out his hand so she had to bring up her eyes to his. 'A stranger you know so much about?'

'When Jonathan was drinking he talked about you all the time. I still don't know if he loved you or hated you.'

'I think no differently about you.'

'What does that mean?' Her lovely eyes blazed.

'Didn't you often tell Jonathan that he had failed you?'

The balmy, evening breeze turned cold. 'If he did, I'm hearing it for the first time.'

He continued to entrap her left hand. 'Jonathan wrote to me constantly from the moment that I first arrived in England.'

'I don't believe it!' Kate burst out.

'Don't look like that. It's true, Kathryn. I have all the letters. All Jonathan could thank about or write about, was you. You must have known he was in despair about you?'

Kate managed a strangled laugh.

'He married you too early. You couldn't have been much more than a child.'

'Of course, you're right!' Kate was furious, but she kept her voice low. 'What are you getting at, Adrian?'

'You and Jonathan. Forgive me, but Jonathan decided very early on in your marriage that you didn't love him.'

'And he wrote to you about this?' Kate asked, astounded.

'I'm sorry if it upsets you, He needed to tell someone. I know Jonathan had problems, Kathryn.'

'Big problems,' she looked back at him unflinchingly, though she was visibly trembling with the force of her emotions. 'Don't speak to me about loyalty, Adrian. I tried very hard, but I would have left him. No doubt he told you about that too?' She felt incredibly hurt and betrayed. Blood was thicker than water after all and Jonathan had been bound to his cousin by family ties, whatever his complex feelings.

'Why would you have left him, Kathryn?' Adrian asked, with no trace of aggression, but rather an apparent desire to understand.

Kate turned her face because she felt like weeping. 'Jonathan was cruel.'

His bronze skin seemed to pale and he stared at her as though spellbound. 'Isn't that a little extreme?'

'Whether he was drinking or not.' Kate put out a hand and touched her son's tousled head. 'It alienated me dreadfully.'

'But I always thought Jonathan hated drink?'

'I think he did,' Kate answered slowly, giving a

defeated little shrug. 'Lots of alcoholics hate drink. Jonathan drank not because he enjoyed it but because he needed it. It's a long story.'

'Couldn't he count on you?'

Kate raised her eyes to his hardened face, 'Oh, you bastard,' she said softly. 'You smug, superior bastard.'

# CHAPTER THREE

For almost a week Cam was very sick indeed and all that time Marcia kept up such a barrage of impotent rage and anxiety Kate felt like screaming from sheer exasperation. To give her her due, Marcia was almost as distressed as Kate by Cam's condition and his heart-tuggingly sick appearance, but somehow she managed to convey that she thought it was all due, somehow, to Kate's mismanagement.

'A faulty diet can cause all sorts of problems,' she told Kate with an admonishing look. 'Cameron could be allergic to some of the foods you give him.'

Kate reserved her shrieks of frustration for when she was on her own. Usually she excused herself and left Marcia unleashing torrents of words on Charles or the family doctor, who pout of the goodness of his heart responded to Marcia's frequent calls.

'It will run its course, my dear,' Doctor Lander comforted Kate. 'It's distressing, I know, but the chances are he'll come out of it during his adolescence.'

If I live so long, Kate thought wryly.

'I don't like it here, Mummy,' Cam moaned fretfully. 'What is Nanna so angry about?'

'She's not angry, darling,' Kate soothed. 'She's terribly upset that you're sick so hurry up and get better.' Before we all go mad, Kate added, silently.

'Peggy said Nanna's a fair tartar.'

'Peggy did?' Kate was shocked.

'Yes.' Cam yawned very deeply and shut his huge, shadowed eyes. 'She was talking to Judy and she said, she's a fair old tartar, that's what she said.'

'Peggy better watch it. She'll get the sack.' Kate plumped up the pillows and lifted Cam a little higher.

'Judy said there were tartars all over.'

'There *are* always extremes, but Nanna is just very worried. Some people talk a lot when they're worried. It's a kind of sharing the burden.'

'I wish Adan would come,' Cam said piteously and deliberately, as Kate well knew.

'He has rung any number of times.'

'I think I'll be a barrister when I grow up.'

'And forget about the police force?' Kate stroked his head.

'Nanna was showing me photos of my Daddy. She started to cry.'

'Poor Nanna.'

'Adan looks like Daddy, doesn't he? 'Course they're cousins. I like Adan.'

Later that night Adrian rang again to enquire after Cam. The sound of his voice always came like an electric current, and Kate was shocked by her own response. He had never been far from her consciousness and it frightened her. She had no wish whatever to come under Adrian Pender's spell. Charm could be a very unmanageable quality and Kate knew only too well how Adrian's hold over his cousin had turned out to be destructive.

When Marcia heard Adrian was coming she gave a brittle laugh. 'Is it to see DCam or to see *you*?'

'Why, Marcia!' Kate looked and sounded taken aback.

'My dear, you're a very beautiful young woman, and Adrian has only ever been interested in fabulous looking creatures.'

'What about Davina Adams?' Kate asked.

'I think he's finding Davina wanting,' Marcia observed without sympathy. 'I really didn't like her attack on you at the dinner party. I think she's nasty under all that Dresden blondeness.'

So Marcia had noticed, even if she had appeared to be paying little attention. Of course any slight on Kate was a slight on the family so Davina would do well to tone down her feelings.

'Adrian has always been brilliant,' Marcia told her. 'Always destined for high places. Wherever Adrian led, Jonathan followed.'

'Adrian said he and Jonathan were the best of companions,' Kate ventured and Marcia gave another one of her brittle laughs.

'Everything Adrian does he excels at. How could my son ever have competed with that?'

Kate sensed the heartache and the underlying deep resentment. It was hardly fair to either boy for Marcia to blame one for his sheer brilliance and the other for not shining in the same way. Jonathan had told her many times that he had been terribly pressured by his mother.

Kate felt a deep quiver of sadness, but she remained silent as Marcia stood up and walked to the high arched windows and looked out at the masses and masses of roses, voluptuous in the soft heat.

'Our families have always been in competition,' she said. 'Olivia and I were friends as girls. She was always more beautiful, more witty, more charming. Even Jonathan wanted to be near his Aunt Olivia. I know it was she who persuaded him to leave home.'

Kate hesitated for a moment, considering what best to say. 'I think it was more because he wanted to find his own feet.'

'Olivia encouraged him to go. Really, my dear, don't try to convince me. Olivia told me to my face many times I was the very picture of a possessive mother.'

'I understand, Marcia,' Kate said. 'It's difficult when one only has one child.'

Marcia's habitual expression of tight concentration gave way to a slight smile. 'What are you staring at, Kathryn? Surely you know what I look like by now?'

'Your face interests me, Marcia,' Kate returned
honestly.

'Such a tribute!'

'Faces do interest me,' Kate said. 'Drawing them is
what I get paid for.'

'That must be a bit of a grind for you.'

'No, I like it,' Kate responded. I'm very grateful
that I have a talent to put to use.'

Marcia shook her shapely head. 'But my dear girl,
you don't have to draw any more.'

'Then how am I going to survive?' Kate asked with
humour. 'I have myself and my son to support.'

'You have a family now,' Marcia corrected.
'Cameron has his family. I was extremely upset when
I found out about Jonathan's precipitate marriage, but
one must come to terms with things as they are. The
way you have conducted yourself since and reared
Cameron does you credit. I certainly don't think you
had a joy-ride with Jonathan. God knows he was
thoroughly at loggerheads with me, his own mother,
for most of his life——' she broke off with a harsh,
choking cough.

'Don't hurt yourself, Marcia,' Kate put out a
compassionate hand. 'Don't let's hurt each other. We
both loved Jonathan, but we couldn't help him. I
tried. I tried every day of our married life and I
prayed hard. It wasn't through me that Jonathan held
himself aloof from you. I've always thought family
important.'

Marcia's ringed hand remained rigid beneath
Kate's. 'I wrote to him many times,' she said
emotionally, 'but he only answered Adrian's letters.'

'Jonathan denied that he corresponded with anyone
from the family.' Kate shook her head in perplexity.

'He always told Adrian every last little thing,'
Marcia murmured without hearing her. 'One with so
much strength of will, the other without it. Is it any

wonder that seeing Adrian upholding all the family traditions, tortures me? You're too young to feel bitter, but I do.'

Kate was playing with Cam in the garden when Adrian arrived. The Jaguar swept up the drive and Cam broke away and began running.

'Cam, please stop, please.' Somehow Kate couldn't bear to see him run to Adrian Pender.

'It's all right, Mummy. I won't run on to the drive.' The adorable, small face was flushed and excited.

'Please, darling.'

The way she spoke halted him. 'What is it, Mummy?' he ran back to her and clasped her hand.

'Let's take it slowly.'

'You like Adan, don't you, Mummy?' The satiny brows puckered.

'Of course I do.' Like! What a hopelessly inadequate word. 'But we don't really know him yet, do we?'

'I hope we know him forever!' Cam exclaimed extravagantly.

It was all very, very odd, Kate thought. Adrian Pender has effortlessly charmed my son, only Cam isn't going to be turned into an adoring little slave. It wasn't any feeling of jealousy that motivated her thoughts, but a deep-rooted determination not to have the past repeat itself.

Adrian was standing beside the car waiting for them. He was beautifully dressed in a dark grey suit with a white collared, grey and white striped shirt and a very classy tie in a subtle shade of red. He was the epitome of male elegance, but beneath the smooth façade was an amazing power—the ability to fascinate and dominate lives.

'Hi, Cameron,' he called easily, and to avoid a tug-of-war, Kate let go of her son's hand.

'Hi, Adan!' he chirruped and skipped across the velvety lawn.

Observing the pleasure with which they met, shaking hands man-to-man, undermined all Kate's calmness. She was, she suddenly realised, afraid of Adrian. It wasn't simply that she didn't want him to exploit a child's vulnerability, it was because her own lines of defence were too thin.

The grey eyes, so startlingly direct, rayed through her body. 'How are you, Kathryn?'

She offered him her hand, though she couldn't suffer him to touch her. 'Well, thank you, Adrian.' With the late afternoon sun falling directly in his face he wasn't like Jonathan at all. He was only himself. A very cool, super-assured, man of character. 'It's very kind of you to call on us. Cam has been so looking forward to your visit.'

He was far too intelligent not to read the faint turmoil of her mind. 'I have a present for him,' he said, after comprehensively studying Kate's face.

'What is it?' Cam sparkled so much he was alight.

'Flippers, a snorkel and a face mask.' Adrian reached into the back seat of the car. 'The days aren't too far off when you and I might want to go exploring.'

Astounded, Cam put his hands to his flushed cheeks. 'Exploring in *deep* water?'

Adrian laughed. 'There's a beautiful world beneath the ocean. One day you'll go to the Great Barrier Reef and its beauty will take your breath away. There are no better corals in the world, and I've explored the magnificent lagoons of Tahiti and Fiji, so I should know. The water is so soft and warm and transparently green and the coral gardens are utterly fascinating. The colours and shapes are fantastic and there are millions of gorgeous little tropical fish. It's another world. Cam. Like being inside a great emerald, all shot with light.'

Cam's small heart was swelling in his breast. 'You mean you'd take me?'

'I intend to,' Adrian said.

'But I'm only little.'

'No, you're not!' Adrian reached out and ruffled the silken head. 'You're a big fellow for four. You'll be six feet by the time you're fourteen.'

'Did you hear that, Mummy?' Cam looked up at his mother with breathless pleasure.

'You'll have to become a good swimmer first.'

'You can swim, though, can't you?' Adrian asked.

'Yes, he can,' Kate answered a little sharply. 'Unfortunately Cam picks up infections from pools and he's too small to tackle the surf.' She didn't need to add, 'Like you did at his age', it sounded in her voice.

'You know Charles had the pool converted to salt water?'

'We're not staying, Adrian,' Kate pointed out.

'You wouldn't take Cam away?'

'We have a home of our own and I have a job to uphold.'

'But we're not going home yet, are we, Mummy?' Cam implored and tugged at her hand.

'Not yet, darling.' She smiled and tweaked his hair.

'We could go sailing at the weekend,' Adrian suggested, seemingly determined to overcome Kate's reluctance.

'Sailing?' Cam was ecstatic.

'Any more magic rabbits to produce out of the hat?' Kate's question was sharp with sarcasm.

Adrian raised an elegant hand as though to ward her off. 'You'd like to come, wouldn't you, Kathryn?'

'Surely you have something else to do?' she cast him a loaded glance.

'Oh, please say yes, Mummy,' Cam begged. 'I've never been sailing in my life.' Incredibly Cam took Adrian's hand and snuggled at his side.

Dear God! They had only just met him yet already he was firmly planted in their lives. Kate tossed her long hair and turned her face into the breeze. Cam was the great joy of her life. There had only ever been the two of them.

'How's it going, Kathryn?' Adrian was eyeing her very keenly when she turned back.

'Fine.' She said spiritedly, as though answering a challenge. 'Are you coming up to the house?'

He looked briefly at his watch. 'I can only stay a few moments. I'm going to be very busy tonight.'

'Miss Adams?' She could have bitten her tongue out after the words flew out.

'Not tonight,' he told her tranquilly, though his silver eyes glinted. 'I'm conducting a few investigations for a client of mine.'

'He can't conduct them himself?'

'Not really. He's in jail.'

'You're a criminal lawyer?' Kate asked in surprise.

'Now why should that shock you?'

'I thought it might have been corporate law,' Kate allowed her glance to wander over his tall, impeccably clad figure. 'There's nothing so messy as the criminal courts, I guess.'

'I majored in criminology for my Masters. It's what interests me now. I may move out of it later on, as my father did. What hope would an accused person have without the best defence?'

'I'll remember that,' she said.

'Now I've aroused your scorn.'

She ignored that jibe completely. 'Do you love your profession?'

'Yes, I do,' he returned smoothly, his eyes never moving from her face. 'I live and breathe the law. It's always been that way. My father used to talk to me about his cases when I was a child.'

'So you knew exactly what you wanted to be. What you had to do?'

'Kathryn, Kathryn,' he murmured mockingly, 'everything you say is charged with extra meaning.'

'Jonathan never had much in the way of encouragement.' Her lovely face clouded.

'Nonsense!' His denial was complete. 'Jonathan sold you a story.'

'And what story did he sell you?'

Cam, who had been sitting on the grass taking his flippers on and off, looked up at the sharpness of his mother's tone and Kate pulled herself together quickly and managed a smile.

'Do you need help, darling?'

'I can do it, Mummy.' Reassured, Cam returned to his highly pleasurable task.

'Did you run away from home, Kathryn?' Adrian now asked sombrely.

'Run away from home?' Her eyes flashed blue fire. 'Wherever did you get that idea from?'

'Answer me.' He seemed unimpressed by her cutting tone.

'We're not in court, are we?' She was so het up her cheeks had flushed to the hue of wild-roses.

'Get it in to your lovely head that I'm not the enemy.'

For him to so acknowledge her beauty was a further attack. 'My parents were killed when I was very young,' she said fierily. 'I lived with my grandmother until she died, and left me alone. Out of sheer loneliness maybe I met and married Jonathan. Does that answer your question?'

'So you weren't a headstrong daughter, but an orphan?'

'What crazy story did Jonathan tell you?' she asked.

Adrian considered this. 'He had a need to mislead people, I think.'

Cam tried to stand up in his flippers and in doing

so fell back on the grass with a little whoop of surprise.

'Here, you need help.' Adrian went to him immediately, and the sight of man and child held Kate mesmerized. She saw the two cousins as boys. Jonathan himself had told her that he had been hopeless at sports and that he simply hadn't been interested. She could just picture the young Adrian with a cricket bat in hand, though. She had been told he excelled at everything. Even Jonathan, in black mockery, had run through the litany of his cousin's successes.

How ghastly it must have been to be forced into competition. A hopeless duel. Jonathan's instability could have been born of frustration and despair. It was easy now to see the basis for his self-destructive quality. He had been paranoid about not keeping her. She, the most loyal and faithful of young wives, had been horrified by his jealous ranting, the urge to violence that had driven her to locking doors against him. Small wonder then, that she could hardly bear the sight of Adrian Pender with his silver, lancing gaze. Because of him, Jonathan had been forever doomed to being second rate.


'Why can't we go?' Cam moaned after Adrian had gone.

'We can go sailing when you're a little better, darling,' Kate explained.

'I'm better *now*!' Cam muttered to himself. 'If you only knew how much I want to go, Mummy.'

'There will be other times, darling,' Kate promised. 'I tell you what—we'll go on a picnic to the beach.'

'Can Adan come?'

'Bother Adan!'

'Don't you like him, Mummy?' Cam leapt up from his chair.

'I think he's perfectly splendid but I'd like to get you some proper sailing gear. A big wind-cheater with Australia Two on it, before we go out with him.'

Cam giggled on order and Kate deftly changed the subject. She was incapable of indifference to Adrian but she'd be damned before she fell under his spell.

It was Cam who reintroduced the subject just as he was saying good night to his grandparents.

'That will be a thrill indeed, young fellow!' Charles Dowling's gaunt face lit up with pleasure. 'Trust Adrian to always think of the right thing.'

'I don't like it at all,' Marcia said anxiously. 'Young children aren't safe out on the bay.'

'My dear,' Charles said mildly, 'there's no cause for concern. Adrian is one of our leading yachtsmen. He wants to please the boy and to make him happy.'

'Well there are safer ways to do it,' Marcia exclaimed. 'I loathe deep water. I'm surprised, Kathryn, that you would want to go.'

'But Nanna!' Cam wailed.

'Dearest boy, you haven't been well. Stay at home with Nanna for a little while.'

The following Saturday afternoon Marcia wafted Cam off to the zoo by way of an alternative to the promised sailing trip, and Kate found herself waiting for Adrian in a distinctly unsettled mood.

'You'll need a light jacket,' he told her, his eyes moving over her striped shirt, white shorts and the plimsolls on her feet. 'It can get cool on the water.'

'I envy you,' Charles told them as they left the house. 'It's a perfect day.'

'How did Cam take going off to the zoo?' Adrian asked her when they were in the car.

'There was a moment when I thought he would refuse to go, but Marcia managed him nicely. She's totally absorbed in her grandson.'

'You couldn't be persuaded to move in with them?'

'No, Adrian,' she said warily. 'I must be in charge of my own home.'

'You have a very independent nature.'

'I have.'

He gave her a swift, sidelong glance. 'That's quite a combination. Beauty and independence. By the way, do you know anything about sailing?'

'Not a thing.'

'Jonathan never taught you?'

Kate could hardly bear to answer. Jonathan had kept her housebound as much as possible, as though any outside activity might make her wish to escape. 'Jonathan preferred me to stay at home,' she said quietly. 'He was rather possessive.'

'Wouldn't you expect a young man to be very jealous of so beautiful a wife?'

'Which somehow transfers all blame to me.'

'Some women are born to fascinate.'

'Jonathan cut me off from my friends.'

'I can't accept that.'

'Then please turn around and take me back,' Her blue eyes flashed. 'I didn't want to come, Adrian.'

'But you did.' He merely touched her with his eyes.

'To please Charles,' she protested. 'He idolises you, as Marcia says.'

'Poor Marcia!' He sighed on a long breath. 'She has a few hang-ups about me. We both try, but we can't make it any different. Marcia wanted a son who was going to make a great career for himself. A son whose glory would reflect upon her in particular. She was very ambitious and she pushed Jonathan too hard. It was a catastrophe. Instead of driving him in, it turned him away from all ambition. How we live to regret the mistakes we make when we're not thinking straight.'

'I know.' It had been her own plight.

'So much for your not wanting to come. Sit back,

Kathryn, and relax. Today you're going to learn to sail. It only needs the two of us.'

When they reached the marina they were greeted on every side.

'Not taking *Sea Fever* out today, are you?' a girl in a very brief bikini called to him from one of the moored yachts. Though she was extraordinarily eye-catching, he barely checked in his stride.

'Not today,' he waved a friendly hand. '*Mirage* is only twenty-six feet long and single masted,' he told Kate. 'She'll do for you to learn on. Come along, Kathryn. The wind is up.'

He threw off the lines that secured the sleek *Mirage* to the jetty and they chugged away under motor power.

'Come over here and take the tiller,' he instructed. 'You're going to steer straight out.'

'I am?' She squared her slim shoulders like a young recruit.

'Nothing to it. You can drive a car.'

Though Kate had never had the opportunity to sail, she loved the sea, so she was only mildly nervous as she took over. It wasn't difficult at all. Adrian cast her only one more glance, then he moved about the boat securing lines and unfurling the mainsail.

She had never seen a man so fit and lean, the muscles in his back and long legs were taut, his every motion strong and graceful. Like her, he wore white shorts and his pale blue shirt was open almost to the waist. He was strikingly handsome.

The mainsail was up and she felt a thrill of excitement watching him fasten the jib. A few moments later he settled himself beside her.

'How's it going?' Somehow his grey eyes caught the blue of the sea and the sky.

'I'm enjoying it.' And she was.

'Cam could have come.'

'I know,' she acknowledged easily, 'but Marcia is nervy about the water.'

'Well it's peaceful today.' He retook the tiller.

With the engine shut off there was no noise but the song of the wind and the slap of the water against the hull.

'When we were kids Jonathan and I used to go sailing all the time. Once we got into trouble in the middle of a storm. I guess that's when Marcia's fears started. I can understand her feelings, but Cam is going to love the water. When I feel tired or jangled I automatically head for the sea. It's a marvellous feeling, just you and the sea and a few friendly seagulls. Let's go after the wind.'

'Why not?' Kate, too, was feeling the exhilaration.

He turned the small yacht and it reared up on its side as it cut across the choppy waves. Above them the sails slapped taut and he called to her over the wind.

'I'm going to bring her about and you're going to help me. Release that line when I give the word. It holds the jib in place, but remember you have to watch the boom. It's going to swing over the boat, so keep well out of its way.'

'Aye, aye, sir.' She moved determinedly, intent in getting it right.

'All the way,' he yelled.

'All the way,' she gritted and released the line as quickly as she could.

Afterwards he gave her his devastating white smile. 'You'll make a fair sailor. Make yourself comfortable while I explain the basic principles involved, then we'll try a few manoeuvres. There are three things to master. Sailing into the wind, sailing across the wind and sailing with the wind . . .'

For the rest of the afternoon they sailed, and Kate found herself improving rapidly. Now she was anticipating his commands, moving in harmony with him so they could gain more speed with a smoother sail. It was an artificial harmony, for they spoke rarely, simply enjoying the wind and the water and the lively sail. The sparkling brilliance of the sea was incredible, changing from a deep blue to a shimmering turquoise near the small islands that dotted the area. Sailing conditions were perfect and Adrian indicated they would anchor off one of the uninhabited small islands.

'Do you want to see it or do you want to go back?'

'See it, of course.' Virgin islands had a magic of their own.

They rowed in to a sheltered cove and Kate discovered that he had brought along a picnic basket containing a selection of supremely delicious things to eat and a bottle of chilled wine.

'Won't we get drowsy if we drink that with all the sun?' Her beautiful skin was already touched with gold.

'I'll sail home.' He uncorked the wine and poured her a glass. 'Welcome to the good life.'

'Thank you, Adrian.' She waited for him to drink with her. On this lush small islet all was quiet and now she was conscious their relationship was moving much too fast. Everything about him was powerful and sudden. He filled her thoughts. She bent her head and pulled her hair out of its tight knot and now it fell forward in deep waves and curls around her face and shoulders. When he didn't have his eyes on her, she didn't feel so trapped.

'I haven't tired you out, have I?' He pushed a couple of cushions behind her.

'Not at all. I feel invigorated. I'm really quite strong.'

'Mmmm!' His gaze slid over her slender body and long legs. 'It hasn't been easy for you rearing Cam alone.'

'I have good friends.'

He leant on his elbow to face her. 'That much I'm sure about.'

'I want to enjoy this,' she said sharply.

'And talking like this threatens you?' His tone was very quiet and firm.

She looked quickly into his crystal clear eyes and away again. 'There's a constant undercurrent between us. We're too close to Jonathan, too close to the past. I don't think it would help either of us ever, to talk.'

'It's worse keeping things in.'

She put down the savoury morsel she had been nibbling and he put out his hand.

'Sorry, Kathryn.'

The touch of his hand on her bare skin was treacherous. Even now, when he had taken it away, she still felt the imprint.

'I'm sure Jonathan lied to you about me,' she said huskily. 'God, if I only knew what he said!'

'You were the only person in the world he ever really cared about,' he told her, his eyes not as gentle as his tone. 'Some of his letters were wonderfully tender.'

Kate's full lips trembled and her eyes were very bright. 'You can't know how—exposed that makes me feel. What right had you to get inside our marriage?'

'Jonathan wanted help, Kathryn.'

'And I wasn't giving it to him?'

'My dear, let's be clear-minded about this. You were scarcely more than a child.'

'I won't listen to this!' She started up very quickly, her dark head thrown back against the sky.

'All right.' He sat back watching her, a half smile upon his face. 'Let's forget it and have a party. I went to a fair amount of trouble to assemble all this.'

She pushed back her heavy, wind-tangled hair. 'You're treacherous.'

He laughed shortly. 'For God's sake.'

'Don't you see the irony of the thing?' She dropped once more to her knees, leaning towards him in a kind of reasoning appeal. 'I had my own life until you pounced on it like a tiger.'

'Next you'll tell me I want to tear you to pieces.' There was a hard twist to his chiselled mouth.

'You could—if you wished to.'

'I've already discovered you're afraid of me.'

She straightened and moved back, her throat turned suddenly dry. What had she expected, coming with him like this?

Catching her expression his voice became casual, the rough edge smoothed away. 'You told everyone at Marcia's dinner party that you thought you had only a slight talent, but I think you're selling yourself short. You should get more seriously involved with what you've got. Something worthwhile might emerge.'

There was a startling depth to the blueness of her eyes. 'I was wondering when you were going to start patronising me,' she said.

'Stop that!' His voice tamed her. 'You know perfectly well it's not true. You want me to put you down, Kathryn, so you can continue to hate me, but I admire you.' He looked up and for a small moment his eyes settled on her mouth.

'So you admire me,' she returned almost furiously.

'I'm only saying that you're doing something now to make money, but you obviously have it in you to gain greater personal satisfaction.'

'I'll remember that when I'm financially secure.' In her anger she poured herself more wine and drank it almost too quickly.

'Kathryn, you're secure already,' he pointed out quietly. 'You're Jonathan's widow. Cameron's mother.'

'Your cousin by marriage. It's like a soap-opera!'

'Why are you getting so angry? Your cheekbones are catching fire.'

'I suppose you've spoken to Charles about a trust fund?' Her clear voice turned caustic.

'I don't need to speak to my uncle about anything,' he told her drily.

'Why has everyone started caring for me now?' she cried emotionally. 'No one cared before.' She gave a despairing little cry and he caught her hand.

'Everyone deeply regrets that, Kathryn. No, don't reject me. No one had any idea you were pregnant with Jonathan's child. You said nothing.'

She twisted against him uselessly. 'I hate you.'

'Stop it.' His voice dropped to a low, husky appeal. What was flowing between them was primitive. 'It's important you accept help now. You're entitled to it, God knows. Assuredly Cameron is.'

'That's right, bring Cam into it.' She broke away at last. 'I don't need help, Adrian. With my *slight* talent I earn good money. Good enough to keep me and my son. I don't want or need your conscience money.'

'Will you stop?' He said it very quietly though something threatening vibrated in his tone.

Ah, yes . . . and you're the one who wanted to talk.'

His hand reached out and gripped her shoulder.

'Don't touch me,' she warned, her mind filled with too many memories of violence.

'Forgive me.' His hand dropped immediately and his handsome face became fastidiously remote. 'If you wanted to, Kathryn, you could give a man hell.'

'You believe it, don't you?' A flame of anger sent her to her feet. She was horrified at the emotions he stirred up in her. She turned on her heel and ran as if she intended to swim for the boat.

'Kathryn!' He came after her so swift-footedly she felt her blood throbbing in fright. 'Don't be such a little fool.'

'Why should I stay with you when you're driving me nuts!' This man could destroy her.

'Kathryn!' He turned her to him while she continued to fend him off.

'Can't you leave me alone?' Pain cut her off. Tearing, searing pain. She gave a strangled scream and he pulled her to him in consternation. 'For God sake, what's wrong?'

'My ankle,' she moaned. Every vestige of colour had drained from her face.

He reached down into the shallow water, catching sight of a translucent pale blue blob. 'It's a jellyfish,' he warned sharply. 'Stand still. I'll get it off.'

'Oh, hurry!'

He tore the creature off with his hands, the stinger tentacles lashing him far more venomously than they had attacked her. Finally he dragged her further back on to the beach, packing handfuls of damp sand around her burning ankle.

'Of all the things to happen!' He looked furiously dismayed.

'It hurts like crazy.' A little speck of blood spurted on her lip as she bit it in a valiant effort not to cry. The sting was incredibly painful, yet he who had taken it on the arms and hands betrayed not the slightest tremor of discomfort.

'I've got vinegar on the boat.' He moved rapidly, seizing up the things they had brought and flinging them in the dinghy. 'Don't fight me, Kathryn,' he told her as he swung her up. 'Vinegar will be a lot more effective than sand.'

Kate clamped her mouth shut. She was just as distressed at his stings, which was downright odd considering how angry he had made her.

The small cabin slept four and he settled her on a bunk and hunted up the bottle of vinegar he always kept on hand. 'How is it now?' His strong, lean hand swept over her lower leg and ankle, drenching the reddened area with the acid fluid.

'If I weren't so damned brave I'd be ill. Put some on yourself.'

'Never mind about me,' he said curtly.

'I hate it when you're so heroic.' Despite herself a few diamond beads clung to her heavy lashes. 'I haven't been stung for years.'

'It was extremely unfortunate.' His hand, that had been moving soothingly over her ankle, slowed and he circled her leg with his lean tanned fingers. 'It's a pity to disfigure such fine skin. You're beautifully made in every way. Was Jonathan your first lover?'

All the pain that was in her, flowed out. 'How can you ask that?'

'I tried not to.' His silver eyes seemed to burn into her. 'Jonathan told me he wasn't the first.'

'Only eighteen and still touched by seduction?' Her voice was frighteningly sad and calm. 'I've only known one man in my life.'

'You enjoy worship from afar?'

'Stop tormenting me, Adrian.'

'It will take your mind off the sting.'

She was shattered to think he had done just that. 'You're wrong about everything,' she said.

'Sometimes I think I am, which means that Jonathan's letters made no sense.'

'Maybe he thought it would make you keep away from me.' She said it in a grave, quiet voice, as though she despaired of making sense of anything Jonathan had ever done or said. 'Imagine what it would have been like,' she shuddered weakly.

'You make it sound as though Jonathan would have killed you,' he said grimly.

'What does it matter?' she shrugged miserably. She had never told anyone about her short married life. She could never tell anyone and thus further darken Jonathan's memory.

'Is that easier?' His silver eyes raked over her downcast face.

'Yes, it is. At least I don't feel like screaming any more.'

'I hate to see you hurt.'

'Then leave me alone.' What did it matter if she wounded him. It had to be.

'That's rather difficult when there's a deep bond between us.'

'Is it Cam now?' she burst out, the tumultuous feelings that were in her putting her in a rage.

'You're really paranoid about your affairs.' His too-intelligent eyes burned like frost. 'I suppose it's even what makes you so fascinating. You're really strange.'

'You won't take Cam from me,' she said passionately and tears filled her eyes.

'That's the most despicable thing you've ever said.'

'Because you're a tiger, that's why!' She was crying in earnest now in mingled pain and apprehension. 'A tiger about to spring.'

'Maybe you're right!' There was a steel edge to his voice and his gaze, that had been brooding, licked into life. 'Did you know that you're one of the few women who can weep with great advantage? It actually enhances your looks. Your eyes are like Delft saucers and your mouth is as voluptuous as a rose.' He took hold of her shoulders, not gripping, but exerting just enough pressure to hold her still. 'But then you're a very sensuous woman altogether, aren't you? Poor, damned Jonathan!'

Muscles bunched along Adrian's lean jaw and the dark, handsome face tautened into sensuality as though a woman were made for a man's pleasure.

'*Stop* it!' Kate gave an anguished little cry and flung herself backwards, but he simply ignored her, gathering her up into his arms as if she were totally compliant instead of flooded with desire and shame.

'Adrian, *no!*'

She might have been begging for her life, but he bent his head, catching up her mouth with such terrifying mastery that her whole body submitted as though it were out of control. She wanted to resist him ... resist him with everything that was in her, but she was so stunned by sensation that it was the ultimate humiliation to have him possess her open mouth.

Emotion without parallel spurted within her, a white heat that transcended the commands of the mind. She wasn't an innocent girl dominated by an experienced man's technique, she had been made love to countless times in the marriage bed. And yet now it counted for ... *nothing.* Even the most intimate of Jonathan's love play had not produced this abandon, so exquisitely and perfectly mind-bending. She dragged her mouth away and threw back her head so his lips trailed a turbulent path down the blue veins of her throat.

'Delilah!' He lifted his head and looked into the limitless blue of her eyes. 'Sirens are born, not made.'

Her head was still thrown back over his arm and she tried to shake it weakly. To think life had led her to this ill-starred moment, to this frantic sensuality, this *extremity.* She had never dreamed so much passion was latent in her flesh. The very fact of her marriage seemed utterly unreal.

'What you took, you stole from me.' Even her voice sounded unfamiliar; ragged, husky, shot through with emotion. 'The last thing I wanted was for you to kiss me.'

'Not on the evidence, my lady. Or the findings.' His face was so mettlesome it looked dangerous. 'You know exactly how to do it.'

'Do what?' she stared up at him.

He laughed harshly. 'Inspire passion, what else? Lots of it. You've had so much practise that you've got it just right.' He put out a finger and brushed it around the outline of her lips. 'But you won't have my head on a plate.'

'Then keep away from me.' She was suddenly half wild with anger. She struggled to break his hold but she wasn't strong enough. 'Keep away!'

# CHAPTER FOUR

THE following week of their stay was filled with luncheons that Marcia had arranged to introduce Kate to a wide circle of friends. The women were all dressed at the height of fashion and a few of them were obviously in competition.

'You'll need a new wardrobe, Kathryn,' Marcia was constrained to point out one evening at dinner, studying Kate's becoming, but relatively inexpensive crêpe de Chine dress.

'That's clear,' Kate agreed. 'I had no idea I'd be leading such a social life.'

'I've been meaning to have a little talk with you, my dear.' Charles accepted a small helping of vegetables from a silver platter and gave Kate a warm look. 'As our daughter-in-law you must be able to buy what you please.'

Kate moved a little so she could touch his arm. 'That's very sweet of you, Charles, but I can rise to a new wardrobe now I've been put on my mettle. I've never seen so many beautifully dressed women as I have this week.'

'They were all trying to impress you ... and one another.' Marcia chose to ignore all signals. 'Your salary could hardly accommodate the kind of spending we mean. Your independence is admirable, Kathryn, but it matters a great deal to us to be able to help you. Charles and I thought we should set up a trust fund for you and Cameron immediately.'

Kate shook her head, speaking as pleasantly as she knew how. 'Both of you—you're too good to me, but honestly, I can cope very well. Naturally, on holiday,

I've let things slide, but I assure you my work is much in demand.'

Marcia flushed and looked a little ruffled, but Charles' tired face creased into a real smile. 'You're a strong girl, Kathryn. Anyone can see that. Strong and independent. I like that. A real mother to your little son. What use is it, though, for me to be a rich man if I'm unable to do something for you? It would please me so much to look after you and our little grandson now.' The light shone on his pronounced facial bones and prematurely silver head. Even his debilitating illness could not completely drain his bred-in-the-bone good looks.

'Charles, I'd rather not accept a large sum of money.' Kate felt adamant about going her own way.

'It belongs to you, Kathryn,' Marcia stressed, obviouly taking offence.

And I could have done with it once, Kate thought and then rejected the bitter unpleasantness. 'How can I put this,' she said soothingly. 'The last thing I want to do is reject your kindness, but it's rather important to me to make my own way, and for me to support my son.'

'Our grandson, please, Kathryn,' Marcia pulled her mouth into an expression of admonition.

'I know modern young women put great emphasis on independence,' Charles said.

'We do, sir,' Kate gave him her lovely smile. 'Please understand.'

'Oh, all right!' Charles responded to her charm. 'We'll forget it. For now.'

'But Charles, dear . . .' Marcia was horrified by her husband's desertion, 'we'll have to insist Cameron be booked into his father's old school. Ordinarily he wouldn't even be accepted because there's such a long waiting list but you can have a word with Hugh Kirkwood. Why you, Leon and Adrian were all top pupils of the college in your time. Jonathan simply wouldn't try,'

'More wine, Kathryn,' Charles asked gallantly, though it was clear Marcia's words had upset him.

'Thank you. It's beautiful.'

Charles attempted to change the subject by discussing the merits of the particular vintage, but it was clear that Marcia had not given up completely. Afterwards she stopped Kate with a strong hand on her arm. 'By the way, Adrian rang earlier this evening to speak to you, but I told him you were a little tired and lying down.'

'I could have spoken to him, Marcia,' Kate said mildly, torn between disapproval of Marcia's high-handedness and the effects of a week of repercussions following her and Adrian's stupendous clash. He had called to the house once to discuss some item of family business with Charles and she had found it difficult to settle even knowing he was in the house. She knew she had flushed on greeting him, but he and Charles couldn't detain her for more than five minutes, despite Charles' efforts.

'I don't think it's quite safe for you becoming friendly with Adrian,' Marcia said. 'You're too close.'

In that way Marcia expressed her wish. She had spotted Kate's and Adrian's unholy attraction for each other and condemned it as entirely unsuitable.

The Saturday night dinner party had now become a ritual and Kate had to make a special trip into the city to buy the dress Marcia would consider appropriate for such a family get-together. Marcia herself was a conservative, but always elegant, dresser and Kate hadn't seen her wear the same dress twice. If it meant going without something, she would have to do Charles and Marcia proud.

The result of her shopping trip was a long narrow skirt in black silk-satin with a simple top in white, made stunning with the shimmer of sequins in a decorative design.

'You're the most beautiful mother in the world!' Cam sat up in bed and told her when she came in to show herself off in the night. 'No one will be able to look at anyone but you.'

'Darling, thank you.' Kate grabbed him and kissed him.

'Don't let me mess your make-up.'

'You won't.' She puckered up her lips and Cam pecked her very sweetly and gently.

'You'll be seeing Adan tonight won't you, Mummy?'

'Yes, I suppose so.' In reality Kate was trying desperately to suppress a feeling of furious excitement.

'You *are*!' Cam gave a crow of delight. 'I spoke to him in the 'phone. Grandpa let me. He's been very busy with his latest brief. He asked how you were and I couldn't tell a lie. I said we were missing him.'

'Is that what you said?' Kate's heart leapt, then plummeted.

'Aren't we? I thought I would tell him. Grandpa told me Adan was always very special. Even when he was little, like me. He said Adan and my father were best friends. He told me all about the funny things they did together. It was like being there. Grandpa told me he loved my father very much and he loves me.'

'Who wouldn't love you, my beautiful boy!' Kate hugged him fiercely. 'Now snuggle up and I'll call in and check on you later on.'

Cam put out a reverent hand and touched his mother's gleaming, curling hair. 'Please—I'm not going to sleep until Adan comes.'

'Did the two of you plan this?'

'I'd hate not to see him.'

There was a knock on the door and Kate swept across the room to answer it.

Adrian was standing on the threshold looking so stunningly handsome in his dinner clothes that Kate had to lower her eyes. 'Good evening, Adrian. Cam just told me you were calling up to say hello.'

'Hello, Adan!' Cam called, starry-eyed when he saw Adrian had a gift-wrapped small box in his hand.

'Hi, there, young fellow.'

'Look at Mummy. Isn't she beautiful?'

'Ravishing!' Adrian made a slight, mocking bow in Kate's direction. 'You're blessed indeed to have such a mother.'

'Oh, I know!' Cam, brilliant-eyed with excitement looked from one face to the other. 'Is that present for me, Adan? Please tell me, I can't bear it.'

'It is,' Adrian went forward and put the parcel into the little boy's hand.

'You'll spoil him, Adrian,' Kate said quietly.

'I doubt that very much.' Adrian watched indulgently as Cam peeled off the wrapping paper to reveal a boxed vintage car model, the renowned Hispano-Suiza.

'Wow!'

'Why not park it on your bedside table and take it for a run in the morning?' Adrian suggested.

'Now I've got two!' Cam told him with huge, round, delighted eyes. 'Mummy bought me a Rolls Royce Phantom I. I never thought Grandpa would have a *real* one.'

'That's a Silver Shadow II.'

'I know. Grandpa told me he couldn't part with it. Look, Mummy, isn't it beautiful?'

Kate smiled gently. 'I must admit they make a lovely collection. Now do as Adrian says, darling, and put it on your bedside table. We must go downstairs now.'

'Thank you so much, Adan,' Cam caught hold of Adrian's black sleeve and pulled him closer. 'If you feel like going sailing at the weekend, I'll come.'

'What about the weekend after?' Adrian promised. 'This weekend I'll be up to my ears in work.'

Kate leaned over the bed and rearranged the pillows. 'Come on now, little man. It's time you were asleep. I'll take that.' She reached for the model car.

'Careful, Mummy.'

'I remember reading that Peter Ustinov thought he was an Hispano-Suiza until he was seven years old,' said Kate on a smile.

'Good night, little pal,' Adrian said gently. 'Pleasant dreams.'

Once out on the gallery, Kate could find nothing more to say.

'You're looking as though nothing mattered more than to escape me,' Adrian said.

'Even Marcia doesn't consider our friendship safe.'

'Indeed?' A faint look of distaste thinned his sculptured mouth. 'Poor Marcia. She should forget all about trying to tamper with fate.'

Most of the guests had arrived by the time they arrived downstairs. They were all assembled in the library enjoying a pre-dinner drink.

'Kate, how lovely you look!' Olivia immediately broke away and walked towards her, holding out her hand. Such warmth and softness were in her face and her eyes that Kate felt an answering glow of pleasure.

'I'll get you a drink, Kathryn,' Adrian said.

A little later Davina Adams arrived. She was wearing an ankle length, twenties style slip-dress that suited her slight, almost breastless figure. Even the sharpness of her expression emphasised the softness of her dress, like icing over something tart. Kate saw her greet Adrian with an extravagant glitter in her eyes then she was making her way towards where Kate and Olivia stood. The neckline of her magnolia silk dress curved in a very low oval and she wore a lovely, opera length string of pearls which she now began to twirl.

'Olivia!'

Kate might not have been there.

'How are you, my dear?' Olivia turned slightly as though to indicate Kate's presence.

'Hello, there, Kathryn,' Davina tacked on with scant grace.

'Good evening,' Kate appeared unaffected. 'They're marvellous pearls.'

'I was hoping someone would comment. Daddy gave them to me.' She held up the string for inspection. 'Don't you care for jewellery yourself, Kathryn?' The very green eyes looked pointedly at Kate's bare throat although she wore the silver leaf studs at her ears.

'I didn't think I needed it. Do you?'

'You look glorious, Kate,' Olivia's laughing face, shadowed. 'I've never seen a more magnificent mane of hair in my life.'

'It's fantastic how far they've come with perming,' Davina said brightly, as if in agreement.

'I don't think anyone mentioned a perm, Davina,' Olivia responded with saccharine sweetness, and then took a sip of her champagne. 'Everything of Kate's is a natural gift.'

Obviously, Kate thought, the only way to deal with Davina was to ace her.

Once again during the evening Davina did her best to make Kate feel like a fish out of water, but tonight, group support was running strongly in Kate's favour. She had been observed very carefully over the short weeks of her stay and the universal opinion was she was a considerable asset to the family, quite apart from her priceless contribution of an heir.

Dinner was superb: a rich oyster bisque followed by beef tournedos with a creamy mushroom sauce and accompanied by a wide selection of vegetables, presented beautifully and with the choice of new season strawberries Romanoff or a very luscious looking chocolate gateau to follow. Everyone adjourned to the drawing-room for coffee and liquers and afterwards someone suggested Kate might entertain them with lightning sketches of the guests. It was Davina, of course, but Kate took it in good part accepting her sketch book and pencils from the young maid, Judy, who had gone to fetch them.

'Show 'er what you can do!' Judy hissed quietly and if Davina had been expecting Kate to fall short of real talent she was in for a disappointment. As an after dinner party treat, the sketching session proved astonishingly popular. Kate had a very real facility for capturing a likeness with a few strokes and a very eminent High Court judge with a reputation for cold brilliance professed himself impressed by her skill.

'You could get yourself a job in the court rooms,' Davina laughingly suggested, though the laugh didn't soften her thin lips. Surprisingly enough she had been avid to have a sketch of herself, now she waved it gently at Adrian. 'Really, darling, is this *me*?'

'It's very good.' Adrian leaned over her shoulder to look. Beside Davina's bone china prettiness his face had a markedly strong and patrician cast. His ebony black hair gleamed in the light and the blackness of his brows and lashes accented the startling silvery shimmer of his eyes and the rich bronze colour of his skin.

'Why, Adrian! Kathryn hasn't done a sketch of you and she's positively staring,' she announced piercingly. 'What about attempting it, Kathryn, or aren't you comfortable with the way Adrian looks?'

Marcia looked around with something like loathing, but Adrian took the sketchbook from Kate's tense fingers. 'I think Kathryn has been kind enough to us all for the night.'

'Hear, hear, my dear!' the High Court judge called out heartily. 'I shall have my sketch framed.'

'So shall I. You clever thing, Kathryn.' Davina slipped off the sofa and clasped Adrian's arm. 'I'm so glad you turned out so well.'

'Don't take any notice of Davina,' Olivia told Kathryn later. 'Sometimes she's incredibly full of malice. Your beauty and charm obviously hasn't captivated her.'

'Why should she feel so strongly?' Kate questioned. 'She's been in the attack from the moment we met.'

'Ah, well . . .' Olivia said vaguely.

'I could allow it to upset me, but I won't.'

'You've got too much character to let her.' Olivia was wearing a long dinner dress in glowing bronze and her appearance was stunning proof of how a woman could retain her beauty almost indefinitely with the help of discipline and caring. 'Have you decided how long you're going to remain with us?' she asked quietly, looking at the younger woman with growing affection.

'I hesitate to put a date on it. Marcia and Charles are so enjoying having Cam.'

'And you, too, my dear,' Olivia confirmed. 'I haven't seen my brother so much at peace for years now. All that grieving for Jonathan. All the pain, all the feelings that one had failed. Believe me, Kathryn, they need you.'

Olivia was studying her, really studying her and Kate held that luminous gaze. 'There's so much I don't understand, Olivia. Will you help me?'

'Haven't I wanted to every day since you came! But we must choose our times. Of course we've been seeing each other frequently here at the house, but I haven't liked to deprive Marcia of your company. She suffers deep depressions from time to time and as a result she's inclined to take offence when nothing further could be intended.'

'I understand.'

A silence fell between them.

'What are you afraid of, Kathryn?' Olivia asked.

'I can't lose my independence. I'm my own woman.'

'Of course, my dear. We all admire you.'

'I must raise Cam as *I* see it.' She lifted her eyes to meet Olivia's. 'Marcia means well, but you really can't have two women in the one house. We don't always see eye to eye.'

'Charles could help you so much. He wants to, he needs to, but you have rights, too. You're Jonathan's widow, the mother of his child.'

Kate sighed and pushed the heavy waves of hair off her shoulder. 'If Cam's grandparents want to leave him something, very well, but as long as I'm alive and well, I would like to support him. I expect I'm over-reacting. I don't know.'

'It must have been a traumatic experience rearing him alone.'

'Yes.' Kate said in a low voice.

'And you had to wait until Adrian came home before you got any help.'

Most of the guests had left in a steady stream before Kate had any private conversation with Adrian.

'Good fortune is with me,' he said drily. 'We seem to be trapped.' Indeed a few people were blocking the doorway. 'When will you look at me, I wonder?'

'Maybe looking at you upsets me.'

He picked up her left hand and she began to shake inside. 'Do I remind you too much of Jonathan?'

'I think perhaps I resent your force of character. May I have my hand back?'

'You don't wear an engagement ring.'

'I lost it.' She lied. Jonathan had promised her a ring, but somehow it had never materialised.

'What was it? Sapphire, diamonds?'

'Why would you want to know?'

'It would seem the only stones to choose. A sapphire for the colour of your eyes and diamonds for their brilliance.' He led her nerveless form through a french window that gave on to the deserted side-terrace. 'The drawing session was a great success tonight.'

Kate felt her blood throbbing with the quickening force of the night breeze. Everything was forgotten with this man. She found him unbearably exciting. To be alone with him was to have their strained relationship get completely out of hand.

'I think perhaps Davina was trying to embarrass me.'

'Then she ought to be in a rage now,' he said very drily. 'You have an extraordinary ability to catch the essence of a subject. That was Sir Lawrence to a tee. He's a cold, hard man, but infernally clever. Even Davina, in her sketch, looked as though she was about to sink her claws into someone.'

'Then what do you see in her?'

'She has never attempted to sink them in me.' He leaned back against the balustrade facing her. 'I do know she has an unfortunate way of speaking when she's jealous.'

'Of *me*?' Kate lifted a delicate dark brow ironically.

'I might have said you're a fabulous looking creature.'

'Marcia told me that you have an eye for that sort of thing.'

'Hmm, I can't help it. Have you ever worked in oils, Kathryn?'

'I should explain that when I'm working I have very little time. I mostly stick to pen and wash, watercolours. I like to work in pastel. I've used acrylics, of course, one can get many colour effects and textures with those, but I've a lot to learn about oil painting techniques.'

'Would you like to be a serious artist?'

The blue blaze was in her eyes. 'Are you trying to pressure me, Adrian, into something better?'

'I'm trying to help you.'

'You mean you will help me whether I want it or not.'

'I was instrumental in bringing you here.'

'Yes.' Her sight cleared and she put her white fingers to her temples. 'Someday, Adrian, when I'm more secure, I'll push my talents a bit further. For now, I have to make money.'

'It doesn't please you to accept your rightful share?'

'I do well enough by myself.'

'Do you?'

Something in his voice made Kate tremble violently.

'We must go inside, Adrian,' she said quickly, but as she went to turn away a large, black moth flew into her hair. 'For heaven's sake!' She tried to shake it out, agitation robbing her of poise.

'Stand still.'

The moth seemed to be meshed in a heavy, deep wave.

'Of all the——'

'Kathryn, *relax*.' He curved one hand over her shoulder and, with the other, gently extracted the frantic velvety creature, holding it for an instant on his finger.

'Thank you,' she said shortly, making the awful mistake of raising her head.

His silver gaze was concentrated on her, bringing the blood flaming to her cheeks. 'Will you sleep well tonight?'

'I will, I promise you.' She looked and sounded highly-strung and hostile, showing all too clearly her intense reaction to his presence.

'You won't have dinner with me some night soon, I suppose?'

'I won't.'

'Do you lack confidence in yourself?'

'Why are you doing this, Adrian?' she challenged him. 'Is it some power complex?'

'Why don't you give your imagination a rest. You're strung almost to breaking point.'

'So are you!' she flung at him. 'There's no cure for some things. I'm astonished you would want to have anything to do with me.'

'Leave it for now,' his handsome face hardened. 'Someone is coming through the doorway.'

It was Davina, deep disapproval in her voice. 'What's taking you so long, Kathryn? We can't go without saying goodbye. Adrian, you're coming on to our place, aren't you?'

'I don't know where you got that idea,' Adrian said dazedly. 'I'm ready for my comfortable bed. This has been a devil of a week.'

'Please—you need only stay an hour. Daddy wants to speak to you about the Chandler project. Some petty official is trying to make trouble for him.'

'An hour then.'

It might have been a promise for all night. Davina rushed to him, incredibly pale and petite against his tall, lean darkness, wrapping her two arms around one of his, tightening, tightening, like slender tentacles against the black cloth of his dinner jacket.

'I really think that sketching tonight might help your career, Kathryn,' she suggested brightly.

'Who knows?' Kate gave a casual shrug. 'I thought that sketch I did of you was quite perceptive.'

Davina inclined her blonde head towards Adrian's shoulder. 'At least Marcia and Charles have given you their blessing.'

'At least?' Adrian's tone was low, but it cut across Davina's very effectively.

'You know what I mean, darling,' she looked up at

him with big-eyed bewilderment. 'It's not as if they gave their blessing to the marriage.'

'Don't be stupid, Davina. You were never stupid before.' His frosted eyes fell directly on her upturned face.

'Forgive me.' Davina looked the very picture of remorse. 'That was rather messy. Kathryn, really, you've vanquished us all. Of course we know Jonathan was infatuated with you. It was just such a terrible pity he would never bring you home.'

'Oh, really, Davina,' Adrian said with deep disgust and she gave a little wailing cry.

'I think it was awful. Poor Kathryn. Now she's proved she is worthy of us all.'

'Compared with you, certainly,' Kate said lightly. 'Don't expend too much sympathy on me, Davina. In spite of everything, I survived well.'

'But I've upset you.' Davina released Adrian's arm and started towards her.

'Not at all, Davina. I didn't attach much importance to what you were saying.'

'It's only that I was trying to understand. It must have hurt you so. Small wonder you want to cash in now.'

Kate stepped back and lifted her chin, but before she could speak Adrian issued an order. 'Go in now, Kathryn. It's quite obvious Davina is prepared to risk a scene.'

'On the contrary,' Kate returned with quiet dignity, 'she would find it very difficult indeed to get my participation. My grandmother, who reared me, was very firm about good manners.'

'Kathryn, please.' Adrian's deep voice was without inflection.

'I'll say good night then. Goodbye, Davina, I'll make sure you're not invited here again for the duration of my stay.'

'What if I won't take no for an answer?' Davina called insolently.

'I'll let Adrian take care of the situation.' Kate moved swiftly through the doorway with no sign of rigidity, but the fluid grace of a dancer. Inside she was trembling violently. Had Davina expressed an opinion that other people might be thinking? She had not been, and had no intention of accepting money. Perhaps Cam was entitled to an inheritance which would be put away until he was well and truly grown up, but there was no way she would lose her own independence.

'Oh, Kathryn. Kathryn, dear . . .' Charles threw out his arm. 'Come and settle this argument. Conder's *Springtime*—whose influence would you say was there?'

It was difficult, but Kathryn rearranged her expression into one of lively interest. Besides, she knew in her heart bringing Cam to his grandparents had made up for a lot of the old misery. By the time Adrian and Davina came in from the terrace she was almost herself.

# CHAPTER FIVE

MARCIA, as Kate now expected, was somewhat jealous that Kate had accepted an invitation to visit Olivia at home.

'You've plenty of time for that, Kathyrn,' she pointed out unsmilingly. 'Why don't you ring up and postpone it for a while?'

'I don't really have all that much time, Marcia,' Kate said, as gently as she knew how. 'I'm a working girl, you know. Not a lady of leisure. I scarcely know myself out of my work-clothes. Commissions are in and soon I'll have to get back to work. Time's money as they say.'

To her horror, Marcia burst into tears.

'Oh, Marcia!' Kate went to her quickly, blaming herself for speaking out. 'I hate to see you upset. Have I said anything so terrible?'

'The young! What do they know about hurting people?' Marcia said. 'Can't you see how selfish you're being? Charles is a rich man and you won't touch a penny. You persist with all this liberation business, talking about *your* independence. It's Cameron who has to be considered here. Next year is his first year of school and we have the right one all picked out. I doubt very much if you could pay the fees.'

'I'd certainly try, Marcia,' Kate said quietly. 'I don't think you realise that successful commercial artists are very well paid. It might be joke money to you, but most people would be happy to earn it. The world doesn't turn on being rich. Riches didn't help Jonathan at all. I have enrolled Cam in an excellent school as a matter of fact.'

'You'd take him away from us?' Formidable Marcia looked pathetically forlorn.

'No, no. Not now.' Kate found herself being trapped. 'I know how much he means to you and Charles. It's obvious I'll have to sell up and settle here. It won't matter so much. I can work anywhere.'

'Work, work, work.' Marcia held her head. 'I don't know that I approve of women with careers.'

'Would you have me be a lay-about?' Kate tried for lightness.

'There's plenty you can do here.' Marcia tried to steady herself. 'All this independence has made you too hard-headed.'

'If I were hard-headed, Marcia, I'd go completely my own way.'

'Yes.' Marcia had to accept it. 'I like your being in the house, Kathryn. We're all getting on very well together. Charles is so much better.'

'Yes, it's marvellous.'

'Now, though, you're running to Olivia. It's inevitable, I suppose.'

'Please don't see it that way, Marcia,' Kate put a hand on the older woman's arm. 'No one can replace you as Cam's grandmother.'

'No, indeed!' Marcia's handsome face lit up. 'I'm thinking of getting him a pony. Could he manage it, do you think?'

'Of course he could.' Kate was delighted. 'What about saving it for Christmas? I should be able to settle my affairs by then.'

'But you couldn't think of leaving us at Christmas?'

Will I ever be free? Kate thought. 'It's a while off,' she smiled. 'Don't worry, Marcia. Now that Cam has found his grandparents, we're going to keep it that way.'

The Pender mansion was pure bliss, like a beautiful comfortable large country house. It was a place where everyone could be happy; adults, children, dogs, indeed Sheba, one of the honey-tempered golden labradors was comfortably installed in a deep flame and chalk-white striped armchair in the garden room.

Cam was delighted and Sheba sprang up to play with him outside.

'What a marvellous house, Olivia,' Kate remarked dreamily. Wide windows opened on a view of the lovely garden where Cam was playing and beyond a small wooden bridge spanning an ornamental pond floating a splendid array of richly fragrant, yellow waterlilies.

'Leon always says it's a world apart,' Olivia nodded approvingly. Neither said that although Marcia was the proud owner of a magnificent home, the emphasis was on order. Marcia did not change the picture or the furniture around and she did not believe in leaving books or personal paraphernalia on sofas or tables. Marcia had made her reputation as a hostess of perfection, but Kate revelled in an atmosphere that allowed for freer expression.

Cam raced about until lunchtime and afterwards he asked if he might swim in the pool.

'I'd feel better if I got in with him,' Kate stood up. 'What a pity I didn't bring a swimsuit.'

'Nothing easier.' Olivia quietened Sheba who was barking hysterically for a continuation of the game. 'We always keep extras for our guests. The pool looks wonderfully inviting to me too, but I've just had my hair done.'

In a guest bedroom, unashamedly feminine and indulgent, Kate selected a costume from the two Olivia had given her; a bikini in lipstick pink and cobalt blue and a black one-piece lycra that actually showed off the body more demandingly than the froth of bikini.

'Oh, Mummy!' Cam cried with childlike directness. 'You can see your bosoms.'

'I've considered that, but there's only you and me.' Kate laughed and ruffled his hair. 'I'll bet I'm first in.' She had decided it was far better for Cam to develop his chest and lungs than agonise over the risks. Swimming was excellent therapy and the pool was brilliantly maintained.

Of course Cam hit the water first, bobbing up and down with excitement. Obviously he thought it wonderful to have his mother in the pool with him and Aunt Olivia had promised him a lovely cold orange drink when he got out.

Olivia lounged in a recliner, watching Kate give her small son a swimming lesson and afterwards when he tired, she hurried him into the house to shower and dress before he became chilled. Kate, however, lingered in the water. At peace. She was floating with her eyes closed when something soft and light landed on her shoulder.

A flower. She flipped up, treading water, her heart jumping violently when she saw Adrian sitting nonchalantly on one of the yellow sun-loungers.

How treacherous was the human body! Against her will she could feel even her nipples tighten, though she managed to call out in just the right tone of voice,

'Don't your clients need you?'

'It's you I wanted to see.'

'Whatever for?'

'What a provocative creature you are! Come out, Kathryn,' he invited, and held up the brilliantly printed sarong Olivia had left for her. 'Don't be coy.'

Kate showed her style. She swam the length of the pool then lifted herself out, walking like an indifferent young goddess towards an admiring mortal.

Not that he was being blatant about it. His shimmering gaze was cool and mocking, but it skimmed her whole body, noting the raised peaks of her breasts, the creamy contours bared by the deep vee-neck and the length of her long slender legs again highlighted by the daring cut of the black swimsuit.

'Pass?' she asked coolly, not even bothering to take the sarong.

'Your body is so beautiful, Kathryn, you should never cover it up.'

He stood up, hard and lean, so much taller than her. Kate moved back and clutched the back of a chair as if from vertigo. It was a revealing movement and she tried to pass it off by throwing back her head and unknotting her hair so it fell in a luxuriant curling mass down her back. 'That was lovely!' she breathed, delaying the moment when she had to turn and face him.

'No wonder men fantasise about women,' he observed lazily. 'Do you ever stop those deliciously languourous little movements?'

'I can't think what you're talking about.' Now she reached for the sarong, tying it around her shoulder.

'Are you sure of that?' His voice was laced with taunting mockery. 'You've been going to very considerable trouble to avoid me.'

'I think you're right.' She sat down and the sarong parted over a long, slender leg.

'Don't you think it abnormal?'

'What's normal about any of this?' Her eyes were as huge and blue as the printed hibiscus on her sarong.

'I had the reasonable hope you wouldn't run away.'

The slow, golden afternoon suddenly speeded up. Everything was moving too fast ... like their relationship. She tore her eyes away, blinking into the sun. 'I don't like this, Adrian. Isn't that clear?'

'Do I remind you so painfully of Jonathan?' He lifted his hand and pushed back an escaping long strand of her hair.

'Please!' Heat was travelling upwards to her brain.

'I'm sorry.' He dropped his hand and sighed deeply. 'You've got to make the decision, Kathryn, to see me for myself.'

'That's awfully difficult,' she lied. He had never been anyone else but himself after the first few frightful seconds. 'What is it you want of me?' she cried defensively. 'Can't we simply be polite when we meet?'

'Don't babble like a fool, Kathryn,' he said grimly, his eyes resting for just a second on the curve of her breast. 'I feel like I've known you forever . . .'

'In a nightmare?'

'Do you feel guilty that you're attracted to me?'

'I'm not attracted to you at all!' She half jumped up.

'Then sit down again. You're not a child. You don't have to start back in terror. My mother is becoming very fond of you. Cam is drawn to me. We can't worry either of them with a silent war. We're part of the same world now.'

'Thanks to you.' Her sudden laugh didn't make sense.

'Let go of the past, Kathryn.'

'Let go of me.'

He put his hands on her shoulders feeling the sudden shudder that shot through her body. 'Nothing is going to happen.'

'You don't believe that!' she cried explosively.

His chiselled mouth twisted. 'Well, not now!'

Every minute she let him touch her she was showing her weakness. She drew the sarong tightly around her slender body and stood up, meeting his eyes defiantly because she knew he had discovered she was afraid. 'I think you're a man who enjoys challenges. It piques you you can't have everything of Jonathan's.'

It was a barb that imbedded itself deeply beneath his skin. His eyes glittered and his dark winged brows drew together in a dangerous frown. 'I've never hit a woman in my life, but you mightn't be quite so lucky.'

'That's all right.' She was elaborately nonchalant. 'I wans't treated all that well in my short married life.'

'What do you mean?' His male formidability was never more pronounced. 'Did Jonathan mistreat you?'

'Don't they all?'

'Who are "they"?' he reacted strongly to the charge.

'Men . . . even you are not so gallant.'

'This is grotesque!' There was a contemptuous coldness in his voice. 'Warnings aren't actions even if you are exerting yourself to drive me to extremes. Men aren't puppets to be wound around your little finger. I don't believe Jonathan would mistreat the woman he loved.'

'Believe what you choose.' She put a finger to the pulsing vein in her throat.

'What about the truth for a change?'

'It would shock you.' She shrugged helplessly, a golden glow emanating from her satiny skin.

'My God!'

'Yes.' She said it vaguely as though no one in the world would believe her and she had come to terms with it. What was the use of bitterness and frustration? 'So don't waste time being prosecutor, jury and judge.'

'Jonathan confided in me all his life.'

She winced at the harshness of his tone. 'So? What a pity you were in England. You could have stopped our marriage and saved me a lot of pain.'

'And Jonathan might not have died.'

One moment she was staring up into his dark, shuttered face, the next she was so sick and giddy she swayed violently and gave a little frightened cry.

'Kathyrn!' He caught her up like a limp, rag doll, looking down into her whitened face. 'I should be shot for saying that.'

'It was nothing terrible,' she cried despairingly,

leaning against him because she had to.

'It was savage.'

'Yes.' His hard chest supported her whirling head. 'But the truth, certainly.'

He tightened his arms around her. 'Something about you make me deaf and blind to caution.'

'We shouldn't be in each other's company.'

'You're safe enough with me.'

'Am I?' A tear slid slowly down her face.

'Kathryn!' Clever and confident as he was, he looked torn.

'I'd pull away only I can't seem to get any strength in my legs.' She was boneless. Helpless in his arms.

'Why do I do this to you?'

'You don't trust me. We can't escape from it.' She lifted her head now, filling her lungs with the freshness of the air.

'Do you feel better?' he asked tensely.

'I won't say no to a cup of tea,' she managed carefully.

'Can you make it inside?'

'Lord, yes.' She put a hand to her tumbled hair. 'You're the only person I know who can reduce me to a dead faint.'

'It's quite insane, having these exchanges.' He searched her face, relieved to see it had regained colour.

'You don't have a very high opinion of me, Adrian.'

'It is never my intention to be unkind to you!' There was a tautness in his handsome face.

'And I don't want to say terrible things to you . Our punishment is, we have to relive the past.'

That meeting, or rather confrontation, weighed heavily on Kathryn's mind in the following days. Marcia had made a good point when she said she and Adrian were too close. She had been over and over her helpless attraction, but there didn't seem any possibility it could become something to build on. Her feelings for Adrian were crazy from the start. He was almost engaged to Davina, if the gossip she had heard was to be believed, and it would be disaster to plunge into a sexual liaison where every consideration was cast aside. He understood that as well as herself. She was sure of it. An affair would be fatal when every day, every hour she relived the fierce passion he had stirred in her with a single kiss.

In reaction, she even accepted a dinner date with one of the eligible men that Marcia had invited to the house. His name was Gil Ralston and he was a director of the family engineering firm.

Cam, not surprisingly, took considerable objection to him. 'You won't go out with Adan. It's not fair.'

'Who said I won't go out with Adrian?' Kate dropped her earring in shock.

'I heard you speaking on the 'phone.'

'But he never asked me, darling.'

'He did. I sort of thought Adan might be my daddy.'

'Cam!' Kate sank down on his bed. 'Don't you remember Adrian is your cousin?'

'I want him to look after you.'

Kate shook her head in wonderment, amazed that her little son should have all these feelings locked away inside. 'Don't you feel Mummy can look after herself?' she asked gently.

'No, you're so beautiful! Grandpa looks after Nanna. Aunt Olivia has Uncle Leon. You're more beautiful than either of them. It's sad you haven't got someone to love you.'

'I have you.'

Cam could find nothing more to say. He leaned forward and hugged her, 'I dodn't know why Nanna invited that man at all.'

Despite everything Kate had a very pleasant evening. Gil, with his thick brown hair and blue eyes, was charming company. The kind of man one could enjoy without becoming hopelessly entangled with.

'You've certainly made Marcia and Charles happy since you've arrived,' he told Kate warmly. 'And Cam is the most delightful child I've ever met.'

How very surprised indeed he would have been to hear Cam's comments.

Cam was still awake when Kate returned home and she found she had to remain with him until he finally settled. 'I rang Adan,' he announced.

'You did what?'

'Adan said so far as he's concerned I can ring him all the time.'

'My goodness!' Kate lowered her head, reflecting on what Cam might have said.

'Adan said not to worry and go to sleep. Gil was a very nice guy.'

'It's a wonder the two of you didn't arrange a little tape-recording of our conversation.'

'I tried to sleep, but I couldn't,' Cam yawned. 'Adan said I must understand you have to go out and enjoy yourself, but I told him Mr Ralston wasn't right.'

'He's a very nice man.' Kate tucked him in firmly.

'Oh.' Cam's huge eyes were round. 'That's what Adan said. You're not cross with me, are you, Mummy?'

'I love you more than anyone, anything, in the world.'

'I don't mind if you love Adan.'

Kate bent and kissed her son's silky forehead. 'It's no good your trying to marry me off, my lad, you're the main man in my life.'

'Anyway,' Cam announced, before sleep finally overcame him, 'Adan is coming over at the weekend.'

Marcia inquired about her evening out, the next morning at breakfast. 'Of course the Ralstons are among our dearest friends. Gil is a dear boy. I've always been fond of him. I expect you'll remarry, Kathryn, one of these days. Who could stop it? You're young and very attractive. Someone has to stop all that liberation. It's gone too far.'

Kate waited until mid-morning before she broached future plans. Marcia was in her study attending to an avalanche of mail and she tapped lightly on the door.

'Could I interrupt for a moment, Marcia?'

'Some days I think I need a secretary.' Marcia sat back and arched her neck.

'I could easily help you.'

'No, no, dear. It's too boring. Where's Cam?'

'Teaching Charles how to play chess,' Kate laughed.

'This house was dead, now it has life and movement. How did we ever live without our dearest grandson?' There was unfamiliar animation in Marcia's smooth, unlined face. Even her eyes were brighter, the expression softened. She had changed a good deal.

'I wanted to talk to you about selling up our cottage. It's small, but in a very trendy area. It should fetch a good price.'

'Never mind about that, dear,' Marcia waved her hand. 'Charles has people to attend to all that. I wouldn't want you to go away and take Cam.'

'I could sell it furnished, I suppose, but there are all our things.'

'Have them professionally packed.'

'Yes, of course, but I'd have to supervise. It wouldn't take me all that much time. Possibly only a day.'

'Then Cam can stay here.'

'It might be best,' Kate agreed. 'Flying doesn't seem to agree with him.'

'W know that now.' Marcia leaned back and stroked

her impeccable chignon. 'If you want more privacy, Kathryn, I thought we could do some remodelling to the west wing.'

'That's kind of you, Marcia,' Kate said, 'but I thought I would try to find something suitable close by.'

'It would cost a fortune!' Marcia snorted. 'This is an exclusive residential area. Even I think what they're charging these days is impossibly expensive.'

'I think I'll look all the same. It would have to be near so I could bring Cam over often to visit.'

'Kathryn, don't.' Marcia pleaded. 'You'll upset Charles dreadfully if you talk about moving out. I've done everything I can to make you happy. Arranging parties so you can meet people. Gil is smitten. I can tell that.'

'I know, and I appreciate what you've done,' Kate said sincerely. 'But I did say at the beginning it was a visit. I really do need a place of my own.'

'What's a few more months to you?' Marcia demanded, becoming rather flushed. 'Of course it's Adrian, isn't it?'

'Adrian?' Kate was devastated.

'He's like a hawk waiting to swoop down and carry you off.'

'Marcia!' Kate protested faintly.

'He thinks he only has to reach out and you'll fall into his arms.'

'Marcia, listen . . .' Kate put out her hand. 'You're exaggerating terribly.'

'Am I?' Marcia's tone was dry and brittle. 'I'm too old to have the wool pulled over my eyes. You're madly attracted to each other and it's no good at all. Why, he's as good as engaged to Davina Adams. They're the same sort of people.'

'You don't really think so.'

'Well he's the only man who could keep her in line.

She thinks she's so clever and she's been spoiled rotten by that father of hers. I'd have taken a hairbrush to her long ago if I were poor Ruth.' Marcia gave a short, mirthless laugh. 'I'd avoid getting in that young woman's way, Kathryn, if I were you. Count yourself a babe in arms when that young lady is around. She'd chop you into little pieces if you tried to take Adrian from her. God knows she's hung in there long enough when she could have been safely married.'

'Olivia says nothing about it at all.'

'Olivia has lost count of all the hearts Adrian has broken. What do you think he's been doing all these years? He's thirty-three. Handsome as the devil, with a brilliant career. He's rich in his own right and he's going to be richer. You don't think Davina is going to give up all that without a fight?'

'That's their affair, Marcia,' Kate said, looking so firm and disinterested Marcia almost sighed in relief. 'One way and other I've had enough trouble. All I want is the quiet life.'

It was not to be. Suddenly she was besieged by invitations to which Marcia and Charles gave their full approval. The more she fitted in, the happier she would be and more loathe to leave. Marcia was particularly kindly disposed towards Gil Ralston who either offered to act as Kate's escort or was certain to be a member of the charmed circle. She went to the opera, ballet, theatre, art showings and parties large and small.

'Kathryn, you can't wear that dress again!' Marcia told her.

'Reinforcements should arrive tomorrow.' Kathryn had in fact flown interstate to arrange the packing and freighting of her personal effects but there had been a minor delay with an industrial dispute. Even so she couldn't hope to compete with most of the women she had come to know. They had to spend a fortune on clothes, shoes, bags, hair-dos and so on, but she had other priorities.

Not to be foiled, Marcia seized the initiative and ordered up an entire wardrobe, claiming she would be bitterly offended if Kate threw a gesture she had every right to make, back in her face.

'Do indulge us just this once, Kate,' Charles begged her. 'We'd be so happy if you would.'

'How could I not?' She was so touched she jumped up and kissed his cheek. 'Marcia has perfect taste.'

'Of course she has! She's a very capable woman. And you'll bring your own vibrant self. If only we'd been together from the beginning. I can't believe it all happened as it did.'

'That's past, Charles.' She sank on to the footstool at his feet. 'Don't talk about it. It upsets you.'

'Jonathan didn't want us to know you. He was my son and I loved him, but one couldn't get past all the defences he threw up. The smokescreens. Marcia worried about the boy so much. She's so quick herself, so she asked too much of him. He wasn't able to give it, you see. In the end, he rebelled. We took the wrong line. In those days I had a very hectic business life so I wasn't around as much as I should have been. My son needed me to get past the disorganised stage. Certain individuals are born to succeed on their own. Others need lots of help and encouragement. Jonathan adopted a kind of bravado but he lacked confidence underneath.'

That night Kate attended at art showing with Gil and, as they approached one of the paintings, a hand reached out and touched Kate's arm.

'Why, Kathryn, what a surprise!'

'Davina.' Kate responded calmly. 'You know Gil, of course.'

'Good to see you, Davina,' Gil responded pleasantly. 'Adrian can't make it?'

'He'll be here!' Davina responded gaily. 'When do you ever see me without Adrian by my side?'

'Actually plenty of times,' Gil whispered to Kate when they had moved away. 'If you ask me Davina has been expending her energies on the wrong man. Adrian discarded her way back, but she fights on. I guess we all have our fantasies.' Proudly he ushered her through the two large rooms. Kate was wearing a stunning creation in three different shades of blue, a long slinky skirt and a luxurious top that plunged rather daringly with full, billowing chiffon sleeves. When Gil had first seen her in it he had swallowed hard, not knowing Marcia had selected it when she had gone on her shopping rampage. Now she looked so beautiful and exotic she was attracting as much attention as any high priced painting that hung on the gallery's walls. Gil was dazzled she had consented to come out with him at all. In fact he was almost drunk with pleasure.

Oddly enough Kate was feeling none of this. She liked Gil and enjoyed his company, but he aroused no sexual response. The naked truth was that no man had ever made her feel like Adrian. Neither Jonathan, nor Adam nor the many men who had admired her. It was all so ironic and she had spent hours and days and weeks agonizing over the situation. She was even beginning to realise it wasn't fair to Gil to invade his life. He had kissed her twice and she had given in to it, partly as an experiment and partly because he was so warm and nice, but she had felt sad afterwards.

Adrian's voice startled her, causing the half filled glass of champagne she was holding, to nearly spill.

'Hello, there,' he said drily, smiling at Gil and eyeing Kate's silky black hair and shimmering dress. 'Am I interrupting something?'

'Not at all!' Gil boomed brightly. 'What a night!

Did you ever see such a crush? If only a tenth would buy something, it would be a sell-out.'

'You look ravishing this evening, Kathryn,' Adrian drawled.

'Does she ever!' Gil raised his glass in response. 'Tighe should capture her on canvas. I'd buy it all right.'

There was a glint in Adrian's eyes and the next instant it was gone. 'Cam told me your private 'phone has never stopped ringing.'

Kate didn't respond and Gil said almost cheerfully. 'Frankly, I don't think the little fellow likes me.'

'It's Kathryn who has the fatal attraction,' said Adrian.

His choice of words jarred Kate, but Gil's smile widened. 'Also true. By the way, congratualations on getting that Romano boy off.'

'He was innocent.' Adrian drew in his nostrils looking, all of a sudden, very cool and arrogant.

'Of course.' Gil just as suddenly sounded nervous. 'Look, you haven't got a drink. Let me get you one. Kathryn, that must be lukewarm.'

'How nice of you,' Adrian smiled.

'My pleasure.' Gil looked like a little boy who had been patted on the head. 'Talk to Kathryn, while I'm away.'

'Thank you, Gil.' Adrian bowed slightly. 'There's a few things I wanted to say.'

'Oh!' Gil blinked twice and turned away.

'I suppose you know you were making him nervous?' Kate accused.

Adrian took her by the arm and drew her aside. 'Vaguely.' He looked into her eyes, as deeply blue as a woman's eyes could ever be. 'Gil's a good guy. Everyone likes him, but maybe Cam has a few complaints.'

'He keeps ringing you?'

'He needs to confide in someone.'

'And who said history never repeats itself?'

'Smile, Kathryn,' he gently warned her. 'So many people are looking in this direction. That dress is so damned sexy you ought to be locked up.'

'Marcia picked it.'

'Really?' He couldn't hold back a laugh. 'Then I've no complaints about Marcia's taste.'

'I don't think she realised it was so dramatic until I put it on.'

His eyes slipped from her face to the cleft of her breasts, stripping her without a word. 'If you have any mercy at all, uninvolve yourself with poor old Gil.'

'Gil will be fine,' she said firmly, though a flush coloured her cheeks.

'There's no question he is now, I'm talking about later when you drop him.'

'Personally I don't believe in interfering in other people's lives.'

'So don't ravage Gil's.'

She stared up at him and the faintest little sob escaped her lips. 'What is it? Loyalty for a friend?'

'Other reasons entirely.'

'Like what?'

'I may want you for myself.'

'You're power-hungry.'

'At this point you might have to be overpowered.'

She had never been more glad of a crowd surrounding her. She was pathetically vulnerable to this man and he was using that knowledge as a weapon.

'How are things with Davina?' In her panic she resorted to aggression.

'I hardly get to see her.'

'It must be tough for her competing with the law.' There was a nervous edge to her clear voice. 'Then again, it would be almost perfect having a member of the same illustrious profession for a wife.'

'You're playing the wrong hunch, Kathryn,' he told her, silver eyes mocking. 'It's not Davina for me and never has been.'

'Then why give her such a rough time?'

'What rubbish.'

The cool contempt in his voice hit her like a slap. Her slender body stiffened and she turned her face away. 'Thank God, Gil's coming.'

'You're always looking for a way out, aren't you?'

'I don't even want to be in the same room as you.'

'Because you can't handle it.'

'I'm sorry, I'm sorry,' Gil smiled apologetically. 'There's such a crush that in the end I had to help myself. One for you, Kathryn and one for Adrian. By the way, Davina and that Kendall woman were searching for you.'

'Then I should go to them immediately.' Adrian turned to Kathryn just for a moment, magnificently arrogant and far and away the handsomest, most elegant man in the room. 'Thank you for entertaining me, Kathryn. You're wonderful company. Tell Cam I'll stop by at the weekend.'

# CHAPTER SIX

KATE had scarcely been in bed an hour when Marcia came to her door, twisting the knob desperately and crying out Kate's name. 'Kathryn, Kathryn, wake up!'

She was awake instantly, slipping out of bed and pulling on her robe. 'Marcia, what is it?'

'It's Charles. I think he's having a heart attack.'

Kate was galvanised into action, though her head went tingly with fright. 'Can you give him his medication? Shouldn't we get the ambulance?'

'Oh, God, God help us!' Marcia slumped against the door, one hand clamped to her mouth as though she were about to be violently ill. 'Charles, Charles, is he dying?'

Kate didn't wait. She flew along the corridor to Charles Dowling's room.

'Grandfather!' She went to him, shocked by the peculiar greyish yellow of his skin, the way his eyes seemed to have shrunk back in his head. 'Your medication.'

'There.' The sound was almost inaudible but Kate followed the direction of his eyes.

She searched frantically through an assortment of bottles. Anginine. Surely that would be it?

'Anginine, Grandfather?' She held up the bottle to his eyes.

Again he answered soundlessly and she shook out a tablet and placed it under his tongue.

'Doctor Lander, Kate.' Marcia was sobbing quietly as though she had lost all hope, all courage. 'Oh, Charles. My poor Charles.'

Kate leafed through the telephone index rapidly.

Her call remained unanswered for long fearful seconds then a man's gruff voice came on the 'phone.

Kate explained very quickly and hung up. 'Marcia, he's coming.'

'Oh, thank God.' Marcia slumped heavily into a high-backed chair that stood by the wall. Approaching the bed was clearly beyond her and Kate marvelled at the way grief took different people.

She sat by the bed and took Charles's hand, relieved to see he was looking fractionally better.

Doctor Lander arrived in record time. He sent both women out of the room and five minutes later emerged to tell them briefly his patient's condition was serious, but not critical. The pain he had been experiencing was not a coronary, but due to blocked arteries. However he suggested they might ring Lady Pender and inform her of her brother's condition.

Amazingly Marcia pulled herself together. 'I'll do it, Kate,' she said, in a ghost of her usual prim tone.

Sir Leon was still out of the state but Olivia and Adrian arrived within minutes of each other, their faces grave. Charles was in a sedated sleep and when they satisfied themselves he was comfortable, they all went down to the library.

'Kate, you're shivering.' Olivia suddenly noticed.

'Reaction, I think. I'm not cold.' She was wearing a Chinese red silk robe with a brilliant bird spreading its wings across her back and around her shoulders, and with her hair cascading around her pale face she looked little more than a very young girl.

'He'll pull through,' Adrian said bracingly. 'This time he has the will to live.'

'He's been getting better every day,' Marcia agonized. 'I begged you not to speak to him about leaving, Kathryn. I begged you.'

'But I didn't speak to him, Marcia!' Kate burst out in terrible dismay. 'I had intended to speak to him but

I was waiting for the appropriate moment. Please believe me.'

'Kate, dearest, we do believe you.' Olivia pressed white fingers to her throbbing temples.

'You're all right, aren't you?' Adrian moved instantly to his mother's side.

'Yes, darling.' She let him take her hands. 'I'm just terribly worried, like the rest of us.'

'He should have the operation.'

'The operation that will kill him?' Marcia cried distractedly.

'It could make him a well man, Marcia, in one giant sweep. If you gave him your support he'd do it, I'm sure.'

'He could die,' Marcia wailed.

Ten minutes later Dr Lander stomped back into the room, biting his lip. 'He ought to have that goddamn operation,' he told them almost angrily. 'Poor old chap!'

'Oh, no!' Marcia put her head in her hands.

'He has a splendid chance, Marcia. That's what I don't seem to be able to get through your head.'

Marcia turned and fled and Olivia with a very strained face moved to go after her. 'I'll talk to her, George. She's so frightened that she might be left all alone.'

Dr Lander laughed harshly. 'She will be if I don't get him into hospital as soon as possible.'

Olivia decided to stay over the night and after the doctor had gone Adrian took Kate's hand and led her to the door. 'Walk down to the car with me.'

'I don't have any shoes on.' Subconsciously she was fighting a powerful compulsion.

'If you think that's going to put me off, you're quite wrong.'

A sharp, wild feeling hung in the air between them, as if the shocking trauma of the night had unleashed emotions better kept under control. 'I wasn't trying to put you off,' she denied.

'There's no law that says you must fear me the way you do.'

'Unfortunately it's happened.'

The sky was studded densely with precious stones and the air was suffused with a heady mixture of gardenias, roses and the spicy scent of the geraniums that trailed profusely over the low, stone wall.

'What exactly is this operation for Charles?' she asked worriedly.

'A triple by-pass. You've heard of it?'

'But that's very serious.'

'Three arteries are involved now. He had a bad bout of rhuematic fever when he was a boy. It left him with a murmur and a damaged valve to the heart. He should have had the operation at least three years ago.'

'But he could die on the operating table!'

'The operation has a very encouraging success rate,' Adrian stressed positively. 'He was going down fast before you and Cam arrived. He must have the operation, Kathryn.'

'I know. It's just I can appreciate Marcia's fears. I see a lot of Jonathan in his mother, you know. Both of them liked to appear super-confident, but there's a terrible insecurity underneath. I suppose you could say Marcia's fears are more for herself than Charles, but that doesn't make them any less real. Even my leaving here has become a highly emotive subject when I made it quite plain I was only coming for a visit.'

'You didn't speak to Charles?'

'I said I didn't. Olivia believed me at once.'

'She did.' He inclined his dark head. 'My mother is becoming very fond of you. In fact it's staggering the reaction you're getting.'

'Here we go again,' she said heatedly. 'Back to the taunts.'

'What is it you find so comforting about Gil?'

'He's not you!' Suddenly realising what she had said, she broke away, going to his car and opening the door. 'I must go inside, Adrian.'

'Well, then, go.' he said impatiently but as she went to circle his tall, lean frame, he suddenly reached out and pinned her around the waist.

'Don't do this, Adrian,' she begged him.

Tension lines tautened his face. 'Why do you bother with so many mechanical words?'

'I mean them, that's why!' She arched back over his arm. 'Whatever this is between us, it's wrong.'

'And what brought you to that insane conclusion?' he demanded curtly folding her closer. 'Are you a Hindu? Do you have to condemn yourself to the funeral pyre?'

'How dare you!' She coiled her hand into a fist and struck out at the hard wall of his chest.

'I find it very easy.' He caught her hand and held it down. 'What is it you're wallowing in—guilt?'

'What is it you're accusing me of?' Her breath was coming in short gasps. She was alight with seething anger and a cruel desire. 'Did Jonathan tell you I was unfaithful? He certainly accused me of it often enough.'

'Why don't you let it out?' he suggested harshly, gaining control over her struggling body and wrestling her out of the light.

'Why would I confide in you?' she said violently. 'You're no Big Brother to me. Don't you insinuate I hurt Jonathan, when your whole relationship crippled him for life.'

'You little fool!' he said cuttingly.

'So why did he blame you?' she cried. 'Trying to measure up to you was the great terror of his life.'

'Kathryn, you are talking absolute nonsense,' he told her with cold certainty.

'Perhaps I am,' she said in a broken voice. 'Don't you see, it's all confusion? The merest contact and all the pain pours out. I was never unfaithful to Jonathan, yet here you are despising me for being an inveterate seductress.'

'And you aren't?' His hand curled through her thick, long hair. 'I remember someone called Adam. Do you know an Adam?'

Her heart almost shuddered to a stop. 'But Adam is a very dear friend of mine. I've known him since I was ten years old.'

'And he couldn't bear it when you married Jonathan?'

'I suppose.' She shook her head wretchedly, feeling the pull of his fingers on her scalp. 'I didn't think. He coped. I never realised he was so much in love with me.'

'My God, you ask me to believe that?' He slid his hand to the nape of her neck. 'You, Kathryn, of the huge sapphire eyes, don't know when a man is madly in love with you?'

'I didn't love him,' she said helplessly. 'It would have been so much better for me if I had.'

'So when did you decide you didn't love Jonathan?'

'Stop it. Stop it!' She couldn't get away from him so she let her head fall forward on his chest. 'I hate the way you hold inquisitions.'

'And it's so easy to avoid them with a woman's wiles.' His hand encircled her slender neck forcing up her head.

'I beg you,' she whispered, but the terrible excitement was rising in her like a flood-tide.

'For what? To make love to you like you want.'

'Oh, Adrian . . . no!'

His mouth covered hers with ravishing slowness, a contemptuous languor that yet urged her cushiony lips to open wider and wider, so his tongue could curl into the moist sweet cavity, clinging, exploring, drawing on a response so profound that her whole body surrendered very suddenly into his arms.

She was drenched in heat, so even her nightdress and the silk robe felt cindered to her skin. He kissed her as though he couldn't possibly get enough of her, the flimsiness of her night clothing so unbearably exciting that his hand sought and found her naked breast, the tips of his fingers caressing the already stimulated nipple.

She felt the violent contractions right to the apex of her body.

'I want you,' he said, urgent to the point of anger.

'It's terrible for me.'

'I'm glad.' Now he bent his head to her body and her heart fluttered right up into her throat.

The sensations were so deep now, so driving that she was swallowed up. There was a terrible feeling of inevitability about it all. As though she had been his prime target since time began.

'Come with me now.' He moulded her to him so she was overwhelmingly aware of his powerful desire.

'I can't. You know I can't.' Yet how could she control this spread of fire? 'Don't you understand what we're doing?'

'God, what a foolish question!' His voice was full bodied with frustration and the elemental male desire to have his way. 'You read about this kind of thing, but you don't really believe it.'

He held the thick black cord of her hair and kept her powerless while he brushed his mouth back and forth across hers. It incited her enough to catch his bottom lip with her teeth, her nails digging into his back.

'Adrian!' There was something merciless about this mating dance. 'Stop. Please stop. I'm not ready for it. I'll never be ready for it. You can't understand.'

'Don't I?' Her breasts were swollen from his touch, but still he wasn't satisfied. His hands moved down over her body and now she was moving into the very eye of the storm. She couldn't let it happen. She couldn't. Where his hands moved, they burned . . .

With an enormous effort she pulled her head away from his assaulting mouth, words spilling from her that even at the height of passion, were calculated to goad him.

'Must you always win?' she cried jaggedly.

He released her with a violent oath, his handsome face hardening to stone. 'It's not a question of winning, Kathryn,' he said starkly. 'Neither of us were under any illusions from the moment we met. We know what we're doing. What we're going to do in the future.'

'You mean, you intend to sleep with me?'

'Forgive me—isn't that what you want?'

How insolent he was! How cruelly, emphatically male. That cool, assured manner masked a man of strong passions.

'The one man I won't let possess me is you,' she said tautly, moving back from him and drawing her robe tightly around her traitorous body.

Even by moonlight she could see the brilliant glitter of his eyes, the way they travelled over her with slow deliberation. 'Tell me what you like,' he said derisively, 'little hypocrite, your body speaks for itself.'

The following afternoon Charles was taken by ambulance to hospital and they all followed to settle him in. The hospital was a private one with an excellent reputation and Charles had a private room on the fourth floor, overlooking a park.

'How wonderfully thoughtful of you, Kate, to bring my little pal here.'

'It's where I want to be, Grandpa.' Cam laid his head very gently on his grandfather's arm.

'Dear boy!' From the curious serenity in his face it was obvious that Charles had called up an inner reserve of strength.

'You have a 'phone to yourself, Grandpa, and a television. You'll be able to watch the *Muppet Show*.'

'I'm extremely pleased about that.' Charles patted his head. 'Just so we don't have to be apart too long I've agreed to have the operation right away.'

'Will it hurt?'

'No, no,' Charles assured the little boy, gallantly. 'I'll be asleep all the time and afterwards you have to come and visit me.'

None of the women could talk for the terrible feeling of anxiety, but to a small child if an adult said, 'Come and visit me later' a happy outcome was assured.

'Do you think I can have a drink out of your water jug, Grandpa?' Cam asked. 'Everything is making me so thirsty.'

Charles nodded his head smilingly and Kate attended to her small son. Matron came along shortly afterwards to shepherd them on their way and Olivia took them all home for coffee because Marcia was desperate to talk.

'He'll be all right, dear, believe me,' Olivia soothed her, but Marcia was inconsolable.

'Thank God, I have Kathryn and my little Cameron with me,' she said despairingly. 'I couldn't face it alone.'

There was no question of leaving now and Kate determined she had better get back to work. The larger of the attic rooms was perfect for a studio. Light spilled into it and there was plenty of room for a play area for Cam. He had inherited his mother's gift for

drawing and noting pleased him more than to work
with his crayons. His chatter didn't disturb her. Kate
always loved him near her and she had the capacity for
tuning out. Indeed she wouldn't have said she was
working at all. Drawing was like breathing. She had
been drawing copiously ever since she could remember. Once it had been her great ambition to go on
with her art studies, to visit Europe and the great
galleries of the world. As an art student at school, her
teacher had treated her almost as an equal.

'There's a lot of ability there,' he had been wont to
say and sometimes Kate thought there was. Other
times she settled for a very real facility. A few of her
pastels of Cam were truly beautiful. One could get
such wonderful effects with the pure pastel colours
and they were an especially suitable medium for the
delicate beauty of children. One of these days she
would like to turn her hand to portraiture. It was her
special interest and it emphasised her ability for
capturing the essence of a subject in a way that was as
mysterious as it was natural.

Everything depended on Charles' recovery. The
operation was scheduled for the following Wednesday
and when that fateful day arrived, Kate left Cam in
Judy's care and accompanied Marcia to the hospital
for the long wait.

'Are you all right, Marcia?' Kate asked concernedly.
Marcia's face looked bloodless and she was literally
wringing her hands.

'Could there be a worse place than a hospital
waiting room?'

'The operating table,' Kate said before she could
help herself. 'Let's pray that he'll be all right.'

Olivia arrived shortly after they had arrived, and
sank down beside them. 'Leon rang me first thing this
morning. He sounded upset. He and Charles have
been friends from their earliest schooldays. Poor

Adrian is in court. It's going to be a long day for him. We're all so terribly anxious but we must leave it in the hands of the good Lord.'

When, some hours later, they saw the surgeon coming towards them his expression was so grave that they all thought something had gone terribly wrong. Olivia grasped Kate's arm as though to brace herself for a terrible blow and Marcia's firm cheeks seemed sunken and drawn.

Summoning the remains of their strength they stood up, but as the surgeon drew nearer, his expression miraculously lightened.

'Tell us, Doctor,' Marcia implored.

The operation had been a complete success. There would be no waiting period to endure. At the end of a couple of weeks Charles would be allowed to go home and begin his convalescence.

'What did I tell you!' Marcia said with one of her lightning switches of mood.

The whole household was on top of the world on their return.

'We've all been waiting and praying,' Ralph, the chauffeur beamed.

Cam raced towards his mother and Kate gathered him into her arms. This was one of the more magical moments of life.

To Kate's total astonishment Adam arrived at the house only a few days after.

'I wanted to surprise you, sweetheart,' he told Kate unnecessarily. 'I missed you and Cam so much that I've accepted a transfer here.'

'Why that's marvellous,' Kate said, half thrilled to see him and half appalled at the possible repercussions.

Marcia, looking very superior in navy-blue silk with her lustrous pearls at her throat, greeted him with polite formality, sitting upright in her chair while they drank the obligatory cup of tea.

'You say you knew my son?' she asked finally, her eyes trained on Adam so disconcertingly he began to shuffle his feet.

'I had that pleasure, Mrs Dowling,' Adam said kindly. It had taken him less than a minute to decide he wasn't in smooth waters.

'But you're a friend of Kathryn's?'

'I've known Katie from the time she came to live with her grandmother, God bless her. What a wonderful woman she was. A grand lady and lots of fun.'

'And you're an accountant?'

'Pretty flat and dull, I suppose, but someone's got to do it. I've been reading about your nephew in all the papers. I guess we'd all like to be the brilliant barrister pleading for a client's life—a real old Rumpole of the Bailey.' Adam laughed. 'Where's Cam?' he asked with enthusiasm. 'I can scarcely wait to see him.'

'Then we'll go and pick him up from nursery school,' Kate promised. 'He's going two mornings a week now, to prepare him for school.'

'He's loving it,' Marcia supplied. 'We were concerned he wasn't seeing enough children. You know, of course, that Kathryn and Cameron are remaining here with us?'

'Actually I've been keeping an eye on Kate's affairs for her,' Adam pointed out. 'I expect to sell the cottage one day soon. There's been a lot of interest.'

'A formidable *grande dame*,' Adam said later. 'My dear, she simply doesn't approve of me. I've never been regarded so searchingly and found so obviously wanting. I expect she frog-marches you all into dinner.'

'Marcia's all right, Adam,' Kate said. 'It's just that she had difficulty unbending.'

'You can say that again!' Adam rolled his eyes to heaven. 'God, I've missed you!'

'I've missed you too. You're a very good friend.'

'And what about the grandfather?'

'He's a dear man. As soon as Cam arrived, he decided he had found plenty to live for. Jonathan's death went very deep with them. Not only the tragic loss of their son, but the way it happened—the waste. We all know even if we won't admit it, that Jonathan was his own worst enemy.'

'My dear, he was downright odd.' Adam's attractive, bony face took on a grim look. 'When I think of the hell he gave you.'

'Don't think of it.'

'And you're hostile to this Pender guy?'

'He's a very dominant personality,' Kate said cautiously.

'I expect among that crew I'd be the riff-raff?'

'Don't be silly,' Kate said almost sharply. 'You're a warm, decent human being.'

'Could I take you to dinner tonight?'

'Tomorrow night,' Kate promised quickly. 'I'm going up to see Charles tonight.'

They arrived at the nursery school a few minutes before Cam was due out and when he caught sight of Adam he ran to him with pleasure.

'My old mate!' Adam chortled, swinging the little boy high in the air. 'You've got so tall and brown in such a very short time.'

'Adan says I'll be six feet.'

'You'll have to excuse me, but who's Adan?'

'Why, Adan!' Cam could barely conceal his astonishment. 'He looks exactly like me.'

'Pender?' Adam queried with a backward look at Kate.

Kate nodded quietly 'It's just as Cam says.'

\* \* \*

'Not the most impressive young man in the world,' was Marcia's opinon.

'He's been a very good friend to me. I don't know how I would have got on without him,' Kate defended.

'Well, you could have come to us, Kathryn, but you chose not to.'

In such a way had Jonathan often turned the tables on Kate.

'If you're going to see Grandfather this afternoon I'll slip up tonight,' Kate offered pleasantly.

'Thank you, dear,' Marcia nodded her head. 'Afterwards I thought I'd take Cameron for a long drive. There are so many lovely places for him to see and we can stop and have afternoon tea. He's such a wonderfully sensitive little fellow. He responds to new experiences. He has a great sense of beauty, as I have. Yes, he's a lot like me.'

Kate worked steadily all the afternoon and greeted them with pleasure when they came in. Cam was full of all the wonderful things he had seen and he was carrying a large box which obviously contained a present.

'It's a model yacht,' he announced with pride. 'Nanna said she supposed I had better learn to sail.

'I guess I can't ignore the fact that all our men do,' Marcia agreed. 'As soon as your Grandpa is on his feet he'll be back to it I'm sure.'

Kate smiled but did not say a word. Marcia was changing slowly, but very much, for the better.

There was so much traffic Kate was a little late getting to the hospital. Cam had wanted to come again but she was very careful to see he never became overtired. Overtiredness in the past had always led to a bronchial attack and he had been mercifully free of his allergies since his bad bout on their arrival. Kate had put it down to the plane flight.

Now Kate hurried up the wide corridor, carrying a dozen beautiful yellow roses she had picked from the garden, and Cam's latest drawing for his grandfather. It was a remarkably good study of the Sydney Opera House seen from the water, with the skyscrapers behind it, the park to the left hand side and four little sailing craft adorning the blue foreground.

'You helped him with that, didn't you?' Marcia had fondly challenged, when she had been shown the finished masterpiece.

'She did not, Nanna," Cam energetically objected. 'I did it all my own self. Just me. Me to Grandpa. Something special.'

'It is indeed, my darling,' Marcia had apologised. 'You must draw something special for me.'

There was no question of it. Cam held the key to both Charles and Marcia's happiness.

Kate was almost at the door of the private room when she heard voices. Adrian's, unmistakably—so beautifully modulated—another man's, and a familiar bird-like tinkle of laughter from a woman's throat.

Davina.

For an instant Kate was tempted to turn around and go. By now she had a horror of Davina with her distasteful sharp aggression. Of course she was tormented with jealousy more than anything else, but even so, civilised people had to tone down their primitive reactions. Jealousy made men and women irrational and dangerous and Kate had barely recovered from a particularly traumatic, tragic marriage.

Nevertheless it would be expecting too much to want a guaranteed healing period. Life remained consistently hectic and an attractive young widow seemed to be uniquely compelling. Kate believed it was because men expected a young widow more likely to go to bed with them sooner. Well, she had left them rethinking that theory.

The voices continued and she leaned back against the wall, her luxuriant hair curling around her face from its centre parting.

'Funny sort of chance, darling,' Davina was saying.

'And yet he's not lying. He was too exhausted to be anything but honest.'

That was Adrian. Even the sound of his voice was enough to send heat waves through her. She was tired of living wth the thought of him. Tired of having him invade her dreams. She wanted ordinary love. Did she? It was unspeakable to be sunk in sensuality. She felt so guilty. Whe didn't she admit it at last? In many ways her marriage had been an unhappy sham, so why couldn't she feel free of her vows?

'Ah, I thought I spotted you!' Adrian came to the door, very tall and elegant, with unholy mockery in his startling eyes.

'I've just arrived.' She kept her magnolia-pale face inscrutable.

'Charles didn't tell me you were coming.'

'He knows that together we're not nice, quiet people.'

'We're not even nice, quiet people apart. You look devastatingly beautiful. I like your hair parted in the centre.'

'So Olivia told me.' It was a bad start, but his line of talking made her unbidden answers fly out uncontrollably.

His eyes narrowed. 'Okay then. So you're wearing it like that for me?'

'I'm afraid not.'

'Kate, my dearest girl!' Charles extended his arms, his fine, drawn face lightning up with pleasure.

'Grandfather.' She bent to kiss him. So much had changed. 'Every day you're looking better and better.'

'It's going to be all right from now on.' He held her hand very gently, as though she was something precious. 'The roses are beautiful. Are they from the bush that grows beside the arched wall?'

'Right in one. And there's a present from Cam. He told me to tell you it's from him to you. Something special.'

Politely, she turned to acknowledge Davina and her father.

Harry Adams was a dynamic looking man of average height and stocky build with shrewd, hazel eyes, prematurely white hair and a smooth, polished manner. Despite the smile Kate considered there wasn't much friendliness in those eyes.

'How are you enjoying your visit?' he now asked.

'Visit, nothing!' Charles exclaimed. 'You don't think we could possibly let her go. Kathryn is here to stay. Make no mistake about that.' He was unrolling Cam's drawing, exclaiming with pride, 'I say, just look at this! There's no doubt he had inherited your talent, my dear. This is excellent—excellent. Harry, take a look . . . Davina.' He turned the drawing around.

'He certainly is good,' Harry Adams agreed immediately.

'The Opera House is recognizable,' Davina smiled. 'Not that drawing will be much use to him when he grows up.'

Nobody answered and very gently Charles folded the drawing up and placed it on his bedside table. 'Please tell him, Kathryn, I love it. I'll get Sister to pin it up. Cam is quite a favourite around here.'

Kate filled a vase with water from the private bathroom and arranged the roses in it, burying her face spontaneously in the softly perfumed petals. When she looked up again, Adrian was studying her, eyes narrowed to diamond chips, head thrown back, his handsome face a study in bronze. There was something very dangerous about his hawklike expression, an intensity that held her motionless, staring back at him in unblinking fascination.

Davina looked from one to the other and gave a laugh so brittle it was almost a crackling sound. 'If I didn't know any better, I'd say Kathryn was scared witless of you, Adrian darling. I've seen the same expression on people's faces when you've got them in the witness box.'

'All I was thinking was how beautiful she is.'

What greater affront could there have been to Davina's ego?

Davina contrived to appear that she took it lightly. 'I'm sure you could make it as a top model, Kathryn. If you didn't have such a rich family.'

'I'm not rich though, remember,' Kate returned casually. 'As a matter of fact,' she glanced back at Charles. 'I'm inundated with work.'

'More greeting cards?' Davina asked.

'Among other things.' Kate wouldn't allow Davina to needle her.

'Thank God Adrian is so acutely observant,' Charles murmured in a heartfelt voice. 'If it hadn't been for him, we might never have had you and Cam in our lives. I can never thank you enough, dear boy. Whenever I've needed you, you've always been there.'

'Well we all need you now,' Adrian told him and pressed his uncle's shoulder. 'More than ever. Don't rule out going sailing over Christmas. Will you ever forget those early days?'

'Never!' Charles Dowling's expression was one of peace. 'This year we must have a dazzling tree for Cam. What we all need in this world is—family.'

'Hear, hear,' Kate seconded quietly and bent to kiss hr father-in-law's cheek.

Harry Adams seemed deeply preoccupied going down in the lift, but Davina kept up her special brand

of chatter which was a curious mixture of vinegar and
honey.

'If you don't have to rush away, Kathryn, why don't
we all go somewhere and have a drink?'

'We'll have to take a raincheck on that, Davina,'
Adrian returned smoothly. 'I promised Olivia I'd take
Kathryn over to see her tonight.' He took hold of
Kate's elbow, cutting off any quick escape.

'Imagine that!' Davina gave away any pretence of
lightness. 'You are coming to dinner tomorrow night?'

'By the way that Forrester chap is coming,' Harry
Adams contributed. 'I'd like you to meet him.
Interesting man.'

'I'll be there,' Adrian promised.

'Good night then.' The tiny lines around Davina's
mouth tightened giving an inkling of what she would
look like in the future. 'I never realised you and Olivia
were so friendly, Kathryn.'

'Mother looks on her as her very own niece,' Adrian
said suavely.

'How cruel you are!' Kate told him after the Adams
had moved off.

'Don't babble, Kathryn.'

'And don't try to cut me down. You can see the
hunger in her eyes.'

'Hell!' he said disgustedly. 'Isn't it a disaster dear
old Gil is so madly attracted to you?'

'I've given him no reason——'

'Shut up.' Adrian wrenched at her arm.

'You're hurting me,' she said firmly.

'The very last thing I'd do. You're pulling against
me.'

'Because I have to go home and I want to avoid
dangerous discussions.'

'Come and see where I live.'

Her heart jumped so wildly it was an actual pain.
'That would be too much like stepping into the tiger's

cage. A hunting tiger at that.' She flashed him an ironic look. 'Sorry.'

'I only want to talk to you. In private.'

'What is there to talk about? Old secrets?'

'Why not? They're in the front of your mind.'

'You won't amuse yourself with me,' she said intensely and her hand trembled in his.

'I have neither the time nor the interest for such things,' he said disdainfully with a faint edge of anger.

'Marcia is expecting me home,' she answered, bound to protect herself.

'Ring her and say you'll be spending some time with me.'

'Strangely, I don't think that would please her.'

'Come off it, Kathryn,' he said cuttingly. 'This has nothing to do with Marcia. You're making any excuse you can to escape and run.'

'Damn you, Adrian!' She broke away from him, her eyes flashing sparks of fury.

'Where is our brave little Kathryn now?'

She continued to walk very swiftly as though a demon dogged her footsteps.

'If only I could liberate your mind as well as your body.' His hand gripped her shoulder and turned her around. 'Don't behave like a schoolgirl, please.'

'Dear, clever Adrian!' she retorted acidly. 'It's your destiny to liberate me is it?'

'Come with me quietly or I swear I'll pick you up and carry you off.'

'It might benefit you actually to be on the other side of the dock. I can see the headlines now. Adrian Pender Q.C. up on assault charge.'

'Queen of the greetings cards behind it all.'

'Oh, you're horrible.'

'But not a rapist. Come with me, Kathryn. We've been wrestling for ten minutes, but it doesn't mean a thing.'

'I fear you, Adrian,' she said with stark simplicity.

'Why?'

Now the tenderness in his tone always turned her heart over. 'I can't think we have any right to a relationship.'

'Because of Jonathan? Because of your unhappy marriage?'

'Weird, isn't it?' she said.

'Loving you obviously bent Jonathan's mind.'

'And you were part of it all.' She bent her head and the tears welled into her eyes.

'I want to hold you,' he said tautly and when she couldn't speak he took the initiative and propelled her towards his car.

Neither of them spoke a word in the car. He drove with his eyes intent on the road, and Kate looked with the utmost misery out the window. The one thing that tormented her more than anything else was that Jonathan had tried desperately to alienate them both from each other.

As soon as the penthouse apartment door closed behind them, she asked for the 'phone.

'Tell Marcia the truth,' he ordered with harsh arrogance.

'I make a poor liar.'

Judy answered the 'phone and after checking Cam was fast asleep Kate left the message she wouldn't be home for an hour or so. It was an easy, pleasant exchange and Kate felt relieved Marcia had not come to the 'phone. Marcia, too, was tormented by comparisons between the two cousins.

'Is everything okay?' Adrian's voice was close, too close.

'You should know, you were listening.' she retorted. She put her handbag down on one of a pair of wonderfully carved Chinese chairs that flanked the rosewood altar table in the small entrance hall. A

marvellous woodblock of a tiger brushing up against a
bamboo tree hung above it and Kate shuddered in
actual shock.

'How extraordinary!' Her hand crept to her throat.

'I didn't want to drive you out of your mind by
telling you it was there.'

'To think I've thought of you as a hunting tiger.'

'How fanciful you are, Kathryn.'

'No, no . . .' she shook her head. 'To have that
mental picture and then to see this exquisite thing is
quite unnerving.'

She moved so that she was right before it. It was a
superb painting.

'Totoyo Hokkei, circa 1820,' he told her. 'You can
almost hear it purring.'

'You can almost see it leaping.'

'I'm glad you like it,' He touched her shoulder
directing her into the large, open plan living-dining-
room, arresting in the cool elegance of its colour
scheme, an excellent foil for a rich collection of
paintings, sculptures and a few beautiful pieces of
antique furniture.

'It expresses your personality.'

'What, the tiger or the room?'

'Both. They give an air of wonderful confidence.
Could that possibly be a Sung vase?'

'It is, but it was left to me by my grandmother.
Collecting Chinese porcelain was her lifelong passion.'

'Then the chairs aren't Ming style at all?'

'No,' he shook his head. 'I came by them because
Olivia couldn't fit them in.'

'Jonathan didn't share your taste.' It had often
surprised her that anyone so beautifully made as
Jonathan should have had no deep aesthetic ap-
preciation. He had never even expressed the slightest
interest in her creative talents.

'Jonathan was a rebel. You know that.'

'Maybe he had much to be rebellious about.' She moved further into the room and sank down into a cream silk upholstered armchair.

'Don't you think we should get off this dangerous topic?'

'Most of us don't want to talk about the most serious, saddest things.'

'You can't really think I determined Jonathan's attitudes to life?' he asked searchingly, standing before her so she had to look up.

'Perhaps you exposed him too early as a light-weight?'

'That's cruel, Kathryn,' he said shortly. 'In fact, it's appalling.'

'Sometimes people don't stir themselves when they know they can never compete.' She leapt to her feet, the skirt of her cobalt silk shantung dress swirling around her long golden legs.

'Then surely the fault lies in them?' He stayed where he was, watching her.

'The fault, the flaw?' She paused in front of a painting. 'Of course it does, but not every young boy is continually forced to measure up.'

'You simply don't know what you're talking about,' he said quietly. 'I spent my youth looking after Jonathan, shielding him. None of us are really to blame, Kathryn, that Jonathan chose to do what he did. Each of us is ultimately responsible for our own character.'

'I know.' Kate dipped her head in acknowledgement of what he was saying. She had tried so hard. What reason had she not to believe so had others? Her life with Jonathan had been unreal as a stage play. Because he wasn't real.

Like a wounded creature she sought the comparative darkness of the small terrace off the main room. The sliding glass door was open, so now she went to stand in its peaceful, leafy ambience with the dazzling panorama of the millions of multi-coloured city lights and the magnificent star-studded heavens. Jonathan and what had happened to him had hurt them all irrevocably.

'Kathryn?' He came behind her, but didn't touch her.

'How beautiful it is here,' she murmured. 'Almost another world.'

'Put the past behind you,' he told her. 'You have a life of your own.'

'If only the past would go away.'

'What is it that's tormenting you so much?' He caught her shoulders and turned her to him.

'He was my husband.'

'And I appreciate your tremendous heartache. As a boy I looked after him devotedly.'

'And he worshipped you,' she said wretchedly.

'Is the agony because you didn't love him?'

'I did.' She threw up her head.

'No, Kate, you didn't!' he told her harshly. 'Jonathan couldn't break the habits of a lifetime. He continued to confide in me. Every moment he spent with you he knew he wasn't loved.'

'How could you!' she was utterly stricken.

'His words, Kathryn, not mine.'

'There's more, isn't there?' she asked brokenly, looking up at him, the grave, implacable expression his face. The face of a judge.

'You told him you were leaving him for another man.'

'I'm devastated by such a lie.'

'Then tell me one thing—who is this Adam? And how is it he's wasted so little time getting back into your life?'

'I—who told you?'

'Charles as it happened. Cam told him. We all tell one another lots of things. Just remember that.'

'I'm sorry, I can't stay here,' she said. 'You enjoy tormenting me.'

The now familiar band of his arm held her prisoner. Anger was burning in both of them, fanned by a joyless yet powerful sexual obsession. Kate felt it in her like a sickness, so even as she stood rigid, she was ravenous for this bruising contact.

'You're talking great nonsense,' he said scornfully. 'You're distressing yourself.'

'My dear Adrian, you thrust this evening on me.' Her blue eyes flashed fires. 'And you know why? You like claiming your victories.'

Even then she wasn't prepared for the breathtaking speed with which he scooped her up off the floor, carrying her back through the living room into the glimmering interior of the master bedroom beyond.

'Why aren't you screaming, Kathryn?' he taunted her.

He all but tossed her on to the wide bed where she made a vivid splash of colour against the lustrous black quilt.

'Now you're showing your true nature,' She twisted quickly and sat up.

'You too, Kate,' he said simply. 'I've never seen a woman look so right on my bed.'

Her eyes met his so fierily they were electric. 'Your arrogance astounds me. You're everything I detest in a man.'

'Except as a lover.'

The unutterable humiliation was that it was true.

'Oh, shut up,' she said in sudden desperation. 'I've told you before, we're like mechanical toys wound up to collide. There's no joy in this. Only darkness and guilt.' She picked up a satin cushion and hugged it to her in a frenzy, as though for protection.

There was no doubt she was suffering and Adrian went on speaking to her in that impossibly tender voice.

'Come here to me, Kate. You're everything in a woman I could possibly want or desire.'

'No,' she said frantically, even as he took her in his arms.

'You are not going to tell me you don't want this?'

'Because you'll destroy me. You're too clever.'

He made a sound that was very soft yet held the menace of that hunting tiger. 'What could you possibly have done that drives you to punishing yourself, punishing me?'

'I did nothing.' She shuddered violently as his hand shaped her breast.

'You were very young.'

She sighed deeply and turned her head sideways. 'Where have you hidden Jonathan's letters?'

'I only kept a few.'

'Couldn't you tell when he was lying?' Within seconds he had her body in a high state of arousal.

'I've met you,' he said sombrely. 'You're the kind of woman to change a man's life. However,' he muttered huskily and bent his dark head to kiss her throat. 'I want you very badly, you beautiful, haunted creature. I won't rest until you're absolutely mine.'

He found her mouth and such unholy joy filled her, her response was stunning.

'Kathryn!' He bent her back almost violently to the bed, the light from the twin bed lamps rippling along the gleaming cobalt of her dress. Desire was such a cataclysmic thing, settling nothing, yet filling the being with tumultuous rapture.

Her arms slid around his neck, her hand shaping in delight the back of his head and his nape, fingertips curving around the whorl of his ear, the hard contour of jaw. There was a fierce rapture in surrender and he was caressing her in a way she had never experienced before, sensual enough to have her blood flaming, sensitive enough to bring the tears to her eyes.

'Kathryn?' He drew back sharply as a tear slid down her cheek to the corner of her mouth. 'What is it? Are you afraid to care for me? Because I'm Jonathan's cousin? Because I remind you of him?'

'That's just it,' she said brokenly. 'I feel as though this is the first time, the——' She broke off, the need to protect herself underlying her refusal to speak freely. How could she possibly say: I feel as though you're the first man, the *only* man, ever to have made love to me. That would be a total negation of her marriage and God knows she couldn't come to terms with that.

'Say it, Kathryn,' he urged her. 'Let it out.'

'You aren't Jonathan.' She shook her head. I no longer even think of him as my lover, she thought wretchedly, but could not say.

His face was hard, even stern. 'And this other man? Who was he?'

She choked on a sudden hysterical little laugh. 'Why, a figment of Jonathan's imagination!'

'So you're going to tell me nothing?' He caught her chin and held her face up to him.

'There's nothing to tell.' Her brilliant blue eyes sparkled with tears. 'What is it to you anyway? Neither of us had a commitment to the other.'

'You'd let any man hold you, kiss you, caress you as I've just done?'

The curt contemptuousness of his tone sparked her to anger. 'Do you want the truth, or what you expect to hear?'

'Let it be the truth.' His gaze dropped to her full, pulsing mouth. 'If that's not too difficult for you to manage.'

'My husband was my only lover.'

He looked at her with a mixture of ruthlessness and despair. 'You simply take my breath away, Kathryn. You're like some richly scented flower the bees can't keep away from and you tell me that? You've only been among us a very short time and you've brought Gil Ralston to his knees, when Gil can draw on dozens of eligible young women. You only turn up at a function or a party and anyone would think you were a celebrated woman. God in heaven, you're designed for love.' He released her abruptly and stood up, every muscle tight.

'Then isn't it odd I'm so chaste?' She spread her hands wearily. 'I'm not pretending, Adrian. I don't even care if you believe me. So far as I'm concerned whatever beauty I have, it's only brought me punishment. You don't trust me. Even Gil thinks I'm playing some infernal game. I don't play games. Intimacy to me is a tremendous commitment. I'm incapable of casual relationship. I bitterly regret what I feel for you, but I know that it's simply a powerful, chemical attraction.'

'How can anything be simple at this level?' Cuttingly he challenged her. 'Why would you want to even utter such drivel? I left you so abruptly because if I didn't, I wouldn't stop. You want me passionately, yet bizarrely it's against your will. I could take you now. Should I? You'd be everything for me, but afterwards you might torment yourself that it had been some terrible, urgent interlude you'd need the help of a psychiatrist to forget.'

'Don't be deceived into thinking I'm weak,' she responded hardily, carefully adjusting her lovely, wrap-over dress, then moving her long slender legs off the bed. 'I'm strong. I've had to be. I've had to survive without husband or family and had to make a new life for myself. I'll tell you something else. I'm quite happy without men. So they want to take me out and make love to me. I just keep saying no. So Jonathan wrote to you saying that I was a nymphomaniac? He told *me* I was frigid.' She turned sharply, trying to find her shoes. 'Jonathan was a divided personality, but I'm whole. So don't think it's just a matter of time before you're going to pounce because I'll resist and scream if you do.'

His handsome face lost its tension and turned sardonic. 'If you're looking for your shoes, I've got them.'

'Give them to me, I'm fed up with playing your games!'

'Come and get them. You're so dazzling when you're angry you should stay angry all the time.'

Without her shoes on, the tall, lean length of him dwarfed her. 'Thank you.' She wouldn't look up at him, but stared fixedly at his hand.

'It seems to me you've had a whole new wardrobe.'

'Yes, I have!' She grabbed her elegant court shoes and flushed as he put out his hand to steady her. 'Marcia insisted my old wardrobe wasn't suitable.'

'I've never seen anyone more beautiful when they discard their dress.' His silver eyes studied her very sensuously though his voice was cool.

'You helped rather a lot though, didn't you?'

'Next time you won't escape, I'm afraid.'

'There won't be a next time, Adrian,' she assured him. 'I intend to go everywhere with a bodyguard.'

# CHAPTER SEVEN

MANY crazy things are said in the heat of anger, but weeks later Kate wished she had never made that remark about a bodyguard.

Adam rang her constantly, and because he had always been so kind to her—indeed had got her started on her career—she knew no way of putting him off, short of terminating their long friendship. Only Adam didn't seem prepared to accept a continuation of their old relationship. Promotion at work and a considerable degree of success with what he was currently doing, apparently made him decide to put up a fight for Kate's hand.

'Faint heart ne'er won fair lady,' he told Kate jokingly, but Kate was none too sure if he was joking at all. Certainly he was displaying a degree of male aggression that she had not encountered in him before.

'Who is this guy?' Gil asked her. 'I know you grew up together, but isn't he kind of annoying?'

At one party they became so heated, Kate thought they would begin to fight.

'Does Adam want to marry you, Mummy?' Cam asked, round-eyed.

'You've got to decide, Kathryn, if you want him around,' Marcia told her sternly. 'He positively glues himself to your side, and really it's the silliest thing you can do. Gill doesn't like it at all.'

Adrian, on the other hand, took one quick look at Adam the first time they met and shed no tears at all. It was almost as though Adam's face and manner said everything Adrian wished to know.

'You like them like that, do you?' he asked Kate

later. 'Willing slaves? I guess the poor devil has given up everything to follow you.'

Kate had not even bothered to answer. It took too much of her strength keeping Adrian at arm's length. It was almost impossible now that Charles was home and the full intelligence unit was working; Adrian, Charles, Cam. It could be explained they were family, but sometimes Kate felt they dogged her every movement. Cam often fell against her, his knees pressing hers with the quiet communication that he didn't really like the way way Gil kissed her cheek on greeting.

'Adan doesn't and he's my favourite person.'

'Listen—what about me?' Kate cupped his face to ask.

'I love you!' Cam always thrust up his face to kiss her. 'But why does Adam have to come here so often? Nanna said we ought to ask him if he wants us to make up a bed on the floor.'

Adam felt none of the adverse vibrations. He was thriving in the role of persistent suitor. In the old days he had never thought of taking her to dine at the most expensive restaurants, but now he was pulling out all the stops. Always calmly conservative, he favoured a better tailor and added an attractively daring touch with his ties. Happiness and a new sense of purpose gave animation to his thin features and Kate often surprised other women looking in his direction.

'You oughtn't to spend so much time on me,' she was moved to point out one night over dinner for two.

'I love you—remember?'

'And I love you too, Adam; but as a brother.'

Adam only rolled his eyes. 'Perhaps if you'd let me make love to you, that would change.'

'I can't see that happening, dear,' Kate warned him.

'I understand, love. You had a hell of a time with Jonathan.' Adam allowed his eyes to fall to the shadowed cleft of Kate's breasts. She was wearing white, very elegant and summery, and for a change she had her hair up. She looked so beautiful he had an appalling ache in his chest.

Despite everything, because their friendship was so long, and they shared so many memories, their outings together were not marred by arguments or fearful emotions. Adam, though he was prepared to die for Kate, was not a man of strong passions or indeed anything like it. He was essentially a gentle, placid man with a good sense of humour and an air of calm response. He was the ideal companion and for Kate an effective additive to dilute her life's drama.

'Pender's a terribly interesting man,' Adam now said, draining his wineglass. 'I never thought I'd like him, but I do. He's marvellous to talk to. Of course comparisons with poor old Jonathan are inescapable, both of them being so maddeningly handsome, but Pender's another person, isn't he? Dynamic, tough. Nearly scared the hell out of me the first time I laid eyes on him. You never did tell me how his likeness to Jonathan affected you?'

'Traumatically,' Kate said briefly.

'I'll bet he has lots of lady friends?' Adam asked affably.

'You've met one.'

'The sharp, pretty blonde. Davina something?'

'That's right.' Kate pulled a slight face. 'Davina Adams. She's a barrister as well.'

'First class all the way!' Adam joked. 'She's no knock-out like you, but she's got style.'

'She took an immediate dislike to me.'

'Why not?' Adam grinned. 'You're everything she's not. Anyway, let's forget them and dance.'

Ten minutes later they were moving back to their table, Kate laughing and Adam steering her gently with two hands at her waist, when Kate felt she had stumbled into some magnetic field. There was a kind of energy in the air and as she focused her gaze swiftly, seeking the source, a ripple shivered down her spine.

It was Adrian's sardonic gaze she encountered and as if that were not enough, she appeared to be the cynosure for all the other eyes at his table. It was impossible to avoid greeting him.

'Kathryn, how are you?' Adrian stood up. 'Adam,' he added smoothly.

Kate flashed a smile around the table. 'Please, don't let us disturb you.' There were six people at the table and four of them she knew.

'Why don't you join us? That would be great,' one of the men invited. Martin something. Kate had met him often.

'Kathryn's ... friend wants her all to himself,' Davina Adams laughed, with a perceptible glint in her green eyes.

'Very much so,' Adam said as they sat down at their own table. 'I didn't want to get classed as a wallflower. Who was the guy with the glasses?'

'Martin something-or-other,' Kate murmured, trying to quieten the heavy slam of her heart. 'How dismal it is that Adrian should come here.'

'Why not, sweetie? It's a free country.' Adam was surprised by the amount of feeling in her voice. 'Did his girlfriend rattle you?'

'She's tried to make that her prime aim in life, but no, she didn't.'

'Was it Pender, then?' Adam signalled for the bill.

'It's part of his training.' Kate couldn't wait to go.

'But he was charming surely?'

'I can't think of anyone quite as charming as Adrian,' Kate said.

'Darling!' Adam looked amazed. 'What a state you're in.'

'Nonsense!' Kate tried a smile.

'But I know you very well. Your cheeks are flushed and your eyes have gone all glittery. It's always puzzled me that you and Pender don't seem to get on.'

'Quite obviously we can't.' Kate almost sighed aloud in relief as the waiter arrived with their bill.

'Are you going to tell me about it?' Adam put the question in the car.

'There's nothing to tell, so let's just forget it.'

Adam turned his head to stare into her face. There was a faint edge to his voice for the very first time. 'The one thing I wasn't prepared for was to see you affected strongly by Jonathan's cousin?'

'You think it odd?'

'I think it's kinky. If you took a picture of the two of them, they'd look like twins.'

'I don't know. I could tell the difference right away.'

'Surely, Katie, you're not attracted to him?' Adam pleaded. 'I was beginning to get anxious about that Ralston guy, but now I think I've missed something vital.'

'Yes . . . there's someone waiting to take our parking spot,' Kate turned her head, trying to divert Adam's attention. 'Let's go, Adam, and thank you for a beautiful meal. It was really good.'

Two days later Kate was delivering a commission to a city agency when she encountered Davina Adams entering the lift.

'Well, hello there!' Davina cried with feigned pleasure. 'Where are you off to?'

'How are you, Davina? Just delivering a commission.'

'Really?' Davina's eyes dropped to the large folder under Kate's arm. 'More of those wide-eyed little kids with curly hair?'

'Not this time,' Kate said lightly. 'Fashion.'

'How clever you are!'

Kate let it pass. 'This is my floor,' she said as the lift slowed.

'Mine too! I only have to drop something off. Why don't we have lunch together? It's about time.'

'I've eaten already.'

'You can't have!' Davina glanced at her watch. 'Accept gracefully, Kathryn. We started off on the wrong foot and I want to make amends.'

'Why?' Kate asked bluntly.

'Why?' Davina gave a high laugh. 'Everything will be much nicer if we're friends.'

'Except you took an immediate dislike to me.'

'Oh, don't get on your high horse, Kathryn,' Davina begged her. 'Life's tough on us women. I'm anxious for us to talk.'

'Well, I could do with a cup of coffee,' Kate mentioned, not wanting to be too obviously rude.

Twenty minutes later they were seated in the Garden Room of a well-known restaurant and Davina was smiling like a kitten fed exclusively on cream. 'Oh, isn't this nice?'

'Very nice,' Kate agreed pleasantly, looking around. 'I'll have something light. I've never been one for eating in the middle of the day.'

'You have to watch your figure, do you?'

It was said with a smile but it sounded like a jibe. 'Always,' Kate said lightly, although her weight seldom varied by more than a pound or two.

'So do I,' Davina answered with a serious, approving stare. 'Of course I'm only a little wisp of a thing compared to you.'

'You are petite.'

'How's the family?' Davina queried when the waitress had taken their order.

'All well, thank God!'

'Why, thank God?'

'Don't you?'

'I'm not really into religion. I expect you all got very serious about Charles.'

'It's quite extraordinary the vast change in him.'

'Indeed it is.' Davina's eyes were so bright and sharp they looked like glass. 'I've always been very fond of Charles,' she confided, 'but Marcia is not an easy woman to know. I mean, she made life almost impossible for poor Jonathan from his earliest days.'

'Were you there?' Kate asked.

'Of course I was!' Davina stared at her in surprise. 'I've known both families all my life. Adrian was always the glittering prize, but Jonathan was a gorgeous creature. He was a little unstable though. How did you come to marry him?'

'I fell in love with him,' Kate said simply.

'Really? I'd feel just so bloody sorry for the girl who married Jonathan. There wasn't much behind those so elegant physical charms, but I expect you found that out?'

'I'd rather not talk about Jonathan, Davina,' Kate said.

'Of course not, dear. It was the soul that was missing. You're so lucky you didn't have to run off and leave him. He'd have made you pay. How's Cameron, your little boy?'

'Very well.' Kate was relieved to see her coffee and sandwiches arrive.

'He's a beautiful child. Doesn't his resemblance to Jonathan make you suffer?'

'Why would I want to banish all trace of my husband from my life? It's right a little boy should look like his father.'

'And what did you feel when you met Jonathan's double?'

'A bit unreal,' Kate said calmly.

'Obviously Jonathan didn't prepare you?'

'He was forever telling me about Adrian. He simply forgot to mention the strong family resemblance.'

'Yes, but Jonathan was never really in Adrian's class. Left to himself, Jonathan probably wouldn't have given a damn about it—he worshipped Adrian— but Marcia has always been a very proud, over-possessive woman. Whatever Adrian did, Marcia wanted her son to go one better, but it just wasn't possible. I expect that's why he left home and he couldn't turn to Adrian. Adrian was in England.' Davina lifted her blonde head, speaking almost to herself, now. 'I thought about him all the time. I wrote to him every other day. It's really terrible isn't it, to love a man so much? Of course there have been other men in my life. I can't help attracting them, but I've always been faithful to Adrian in my mind.'

'You've told him how much you love him?' Kate was consumed by an awful kind of pity.

'Of course. I grew up loving him. I'll never change. He's always had his career, you see. I told him if he didn't marry me, I'd go off and marry someone else, but he knows I'll never be free of him. When we're alone together I realise how important I am to him, and anyway he's the one who has suddenly reintroduced the talk of marriage. The time's right.'

'Davina, I don't want to be rude,' Kate said quickly, 'but I must go.'

'I haven't said anything to upset you, have I?' Davina asked hopefully, and lifted a small hand to her throat.

'Not at all.' Kate put money down on the table and leapt to her feet. 'You carry on. That salad looks very nice.'

'How can we talk,' Davina challenged her, 'when you want to rush away?'

'I can only say I have things to do.'

'Bosh!' Davina returned rudely. 'My impression is

you can hardly stand my talking about Adrian. Attracted to him, aren't you? One can hardly blame you. It happens all the time. I'm against leaving people in the dark. Adrian is mine. It's something he won't tell you but it's true all the same.

Later on that day, towards evening, Adrian arrived with some legal papers for Charles to sign. Kate was coming down the stairs just as he arrived, and as usual he greeted her with mocking formality.

'Cousin Kathryn.'

'Oh, Adrian.' Her heart began to beat violently, sadly.

'How pleasant to catch you alone for a few moments.'

'I think Charles is in the study.'

'Didn't you just hear what I said?'

'Certainly, but I didn't think I should detain you.'

'Where's Cam?' he asked abruptly.

'He went on a long tramp, this afternoon, with his grandfather so he had an early tea and fell into bed.'

'I thought he might have liked to stay up on the odd night his mother is at home. I gather you are at home for the evening or is one of your admirers due to show up?'

Kate nearly jumped when Charles came out of the library behind them. 'Ah, there you are, Adrian. I thought I heard your voice.'

'I was just seizing a moment with Kathryn,' Adrian announced sardonically.

'I see,' Charles smiled. 'You are going to stay to dinner, aren't you?'

'If I'm asked.'

'It's fortunate you found us all together,' Charles told him with pleasure. 'Kate has been promising herself a quiet night.'

Dinner was early, because Marcia was going on to a

celebrity concert with a friend, but scarcely had they settled before Marcia was called to the 'phone.

'I hope everything is all right,' Charles said, attacking his roast lamb with gusto. 'Helen's daughter-in-law is due to have her baby any day.'

When Marcia came back it was all too apparent there was some kind of emergency. 'That was Helen,' she confirmed. 'She won't be able to go tonight. Jennifer has developed complications. They're delivering the baby by Caesarian. Helen is picking me up on her way to the hospital. I felt I really ought to go with her.'

'Which hospital?' Charles asked.

Marcia told him worriedly, picking up her knife and fork and making swift inroads on her meal. 'She'll be here in about thirty minutes. I just hope everything will be all right. It's her first grandchild and Jennifer is a dear girl.'

'She'll have the best doctors,' Charles said reassuringly. 'Why don't you and Adrian make use of those tickets, Kate? They were very hard to come by and I know you both love violin concertos.'

'You're very welcome to them,' Marcia duly said. 'Five rows from the front. Now, you'll have to excuse me. I have one or two things to do before Helen arrives . . .'

'Manoeuvred into that, weren't you?' Adrian observed drily in the car on their way to the concert hall.

'Thanks to Charles,' Kate agreed with a fluttering sigh. 'It's truly touching his devotion to you.'

'And he's become marvellously fond of you,' he glanced at her briefly and then turned his glance back to the road.

'I think it's an advanced case of trying to throw two people together.'

'What a pity, Kathryn. Romance is lost on you.'

An internationally famous violinist, a guest soloist with the orchestra, was performing one of Kate's favourite violin concertos, the Bruch. They had exceptionally good seats in the magnificent auditorium and Kate relaxed, allowing the music to diminish the tensions inside her. It wasn't all that easy with Adrian beside her, his arm brushing hers, his long lean beautifully shaped hands beneath her constant glance. How could she possibly forget the erotic frenzy they aroused in her? She trembled in remembrance, and as she did so his eyes immediately looked towards her, one black eyebrow tilting with mocking inquiry. She had tried to smile casually, but so lucid was his expression she would swear he could divine every thought that passed through her head. In fact there was answering tension in the lean body beside her. Instead of being overwhelmed by the meltingly beautiful music, in reality they were concentrated on one another.

In the interval he caught her fingers, impatiently leading her outside. There was a large crowd, but he began to whisk her through it with the same silken smoothness that he manoeuvred his car.

'Where on earth are we going? We're not going back?'

'How observant of you, Kathryn. I think we're both wasting time.'

'Adrian!' She pulled to a halt then, though he still held her hand.

'Surely you said it out loud?'

'What?' She opened wide her dazzlingly blue eyes.

'Take me back to the apartment.'

'I beg your pardon. I never even thought it.'

'What a hypocrite you are when you want to be. I want to make love to you, Kathryn. In fact I'm going to.'

'Are you threatening me?' She drew a deep breath,

forced to go with him because he was propelling her too fast.

'Why would I have to do that? You might be an excellent liar, Kathryn, but I can feel every little tremor that runs through your body. You don't have to deny yourself to me for the rest of your life. You'd be suffering stupidly and I certainly won't tolerate it.'

He unlocked his car on the passenger side and very firmly put her in. The moment he walked away Kathryn attempted to get out, but he had foiled her little plan by re-engaging the lock.

'Nobody cares, Kathryn,' he told her, when he was seated in the car. 'Scream away.'

'How can you do this? You're supposed to be committed to upholding the law.'

'Quite right.' He reversed the car expertly in the confined parking lot and headed for the street. 'But far better to abduct you than have this situation run on. I mean, your Adam is so tenacious and Gil only just recently expressed the notion it was about time he settled down. I can't just leave you wrecking lives.'

'You could mind your own business,' she said heatedly, and put up her hand to her blazing cheeks.

'Do you want to marry Gil?' he asked politely.

'Don't be ridiculous.'

'There, it's just as I said. Beautiful women tend to make a mess of lives.'

'Such a thing has never been discussed.'

'Darling—he's getting around to it,' he told her drily. 'You can't attach much importance to the overwhelming effect of your charms.'

A silver Volvo shot out of a side street and he swore gently beneath his breath. 'Only a few minutes more, Kathryn.'

She fell speechless, hugging her arms to her body. The minute she was able to, she intended to escape. She wasn't a helpless puppet impelled towards a predestined fate. She had to fight this thing. She was so terribly afraid. All her life she had had her emotions pretty well under control, but Adrian's effect on her was unpredictable and dangerous.

At his apartment block, someone shouted a greeting—a man—and when Adrian got out momentarily to respond Kate saw her chance. She turned and fled, dodging through a secluded part of the apartment's gardens and coming out on a side street. Her heart was hammering but she couldn't rest and gather her strength. Adrian would come after her. Of that she was sure.

She ran on resolutely, only wishing she had money on her. As she passed under a large tree a hand shot out and grabbed her arm.

'Who are you runnin' from, dolly?'

There are fears. And fears. Kate was shocked rigid. 'Get your hand off my arm.'

'Had a little fight with your boyfriend, eh?'

She could only catch a fleeting glimpse of his face, young and very strong, hidden in the shadows. 'Would you please let my arm go? If you don't, I'll scream.'

'Why would I let you go when you could be what I'm searching for? You're right pretty.'

There was always chance to alter one's world. This creature was terrible and Kate flung up her hand and tried pushing him away.

'Don't pick a fight with me, sweetheart. It would be a ridiculous thing to do.'

She didn't hesitate, but screamed, a long throbbing cry that made her assailant curse violently and clamp a hand across her mouth. 'Now you're bein' stupid, see. I'm not gonna hurt yah.'

Kate didn't listen, but kicked backwards and the man caught his foot on an exposed root of the big, shady tree and they both toppled sideways.

'Women, they terrify me,' Kate's assailant said.

'Then you ought not attack them.'

What had begun sickly was almost turning into a joke. 'Let's have a drink,' he now said amazingly.

He only got half way to his feet because a tall, dark shape leapt out of the shadows pouncing on the man and pinning him back against the tree like a rabbit.

'Kathryn?'

Kate had never heard that tone of voice. It was the sort of voice to make the most hardened criminal quake. 'I'm all right.'

'You'll need to be.'

'Are you kiddin', mister? She's all right. Never touched her.'

'What's your name? Where do you come from?' Adrian hit him with a string of questions, all the time holding him to the tree.

Panic set in. 'All I done was ask 'er who she was runnin' from. Holy cow, mister, do you think I'm a rapist?'

'I believe I'll check that out.'

'Are you the cops?' the man cried. 'You've got nuthin' on me. I'm only here because I was guaranteed a job, I swear it.'

'Let him go, Adrian, please,' Kate begged. 'He did ask me if I wanted a drink.'

'Sure!' the man cheered up. 'I've never hurt a woman in my life, but I don't like the pretty ones to get away.'

'All right then,' Adrian thumped him just hard enough to make him slump. 'If you're mixed up in even a hint of trouble I'll find you.'

The man's back straightened. He took another look at Adrian's frowning face, the hard, lean athletic body and backed away. 'You won't find anything, I promise. I'm just a quiet, country boy.'

When he had disappeared, Kate's mouth suddenly turned dry.

'Are you all right?' Adrian asked curtly.

'Of course.'

'Then why the scream?'

'I always expect the worst and act on it.'

'It usually happens when a woman takes to the lonely streets.'

'Well, I've learned my lesson.' Now that it was over, she found herself quite shaky.

'I never knew you were quite such a fool.'

'And you're as violent as any gangster. Did you have to thump the poor devil?'

'I might have killed him had he hurt you.'

Her knees suddenly buckled. 'Please ... I can see that I've upset you and I'm sorry. It was foolish, I agree.'

Almost angrily he wrapped an arm around her waist.

'Can you walk?'

'In a moment,' she said softly, her agitation now showing. 'I suppose the man who called out to you thought you were out with a lunatic?'

'I'd give that a definite yes.'

'I must have embarrassed you.'

'Not must, have, Kathryn. You damned well did. Can I convey to you what's it like? A woman fleeing me in terror? I believe you got what you deserved.'

'Then why did you settle on the poor devil like some fiend from hell?'

'I suppose I was angry. It was that spontaneous little scream.' He pulled her to him staring down into her face. 'Are those your teeth chattering?'

'Wouldn't yours be under the same circumstances?'

'It's a miracle that wasn't a worse experience.'

'I suppose so. He fancied me.'

'And I won't even attempt to describe my feelings.' He put his arm around her, half supporting her. 'Sometimes I think you're mentally deficient.'

In the light of the apartment she saw that her stockings were full of runs. 'Oh!' she touched her knees.

'Hard to avoid that sort of thing when you hare off like a perfect fool.'

'You mean the streets are so hideously full of men preying on unsuspecting women.'

'Those stockings are ruined,' he said abruptly. 'Such a pity when you were a picture of glamour and elegance.'

'You're a patronising devil, aren't you?' From anxiously inspecting her legs Kate looked up to search his eyes.

The effect was stunning, causing her to put her hand to her throat instinctively. His reaction to her was showing all too clearly in the sensual curve to his mouth and the slight flare of his finely cut nostrils. The voice might be coolly arrogant, but what he really wanted was for her to satisfy an underlying passionate nature.

'Don't look like that,' he drawled. 'I'm not going to swoop on you.'

'I know about you.'

'Tell me.' He leaned forward and slid an arm around her waist, the crystal brilliance of his eyes dazzling.

'From the time we met you've been trying to manipulate me into this.'

'Kathryn, you're wrong.' Slowly he undid the zipper of her narrow, shirred blue jersey dress so it fell away from her creamy back and dipped in a low oval over her breasts. 'What has happened between us is a natural phenomenon.'

'But I can't bear it. Don't you see?' Even then she was arching slightly so her breasts were nearer his mouth.

'I know you want me.' He slid the dress from her

with practised skill, his hands warm on her trembling flesh. 'Very badly.'

She had begun the evening rebelliously, now every form of protest was caught in her throat. With deliberate slowness he bent his head and kissed the scented, shadowed cleft between her breasts and when she gave a soft, husky little moan, his hands suddenly wrapped her tightly ... so tightly that he could feel the pulsing nerves beneath her skin.

'Come with me, Kathryn ... please.'

She couldn't whisper one word, her body communicating her urgent need and he scooped her up, almost fiercely and carried her through to his bedroom.

'You taste of peaches.' He leaned over her, parting her cushiony lips with the tip of his tongue.

Excitement and desire was as sharp as a knife in her, yet she half rolled away flinging out a hand to the other side of the wide bed.

'I want to see you.' To add to the downlight on a single, magnificent seascape he turned on the twin bedside lamps.

'I might hate you in the end.'

'No, darling. You're young and very beautiful and you need so badly to be loved.'

'And what if I should fall pregnant?' she cried out, unable to prevent it. 'I'm not prepared for any of this, Adrian.'

'You mean that?' His dark, handsome face tautened and his voice took on a hard edge.

'Of course I mean it!' She sat up, quaking with indignation. Her blue eyes blazed like sapphires and her hair fanned around her flushed face like a thick, silky-black aureola. One of the ribbon straps of her bra and her glistening champagne coloured slip had fallen off one shoulder accenting the swell of her breast so even a saint could have been incited to ravish her. 'Did you think I was always ready for some sexual encounter?'

'You should be!' he returned with a harsh indrawn breath. 'What about Adam? Wasn't he your lover?'

Fury convulsed her. She leapt towards him so quickly she felt a snapping pain in her neck. 'Adam was never my lover.'

'You were inseparable before you married.' Somehow he had her lying back against him with her wrists pinned. 'He's back in your life now. You ask me to believe he has never made love to you?'

'He's my *friend*!' she hissed impotently. 'Can't a woman have a friend?'

'Not you, Kathryn,' he told her with hard authority. 'He's in love with you. Don't attempt to deny that. The way he looks at you is proof enough. The poor devil has loved you for years.'

'I thought the question was, had we slept together?' She arched her throat back, staring fixedly at the ceiling. 'Do you think I'm going to break like some poor creature you badger in court?'

'Tell me.' He lowered her on to the cushions with gentle force, his gaze fixing on her hair as it picked up the iridescent sheen of the blue satin.

'You have no right to question me at all.'

'And you so obviously prefer not to answer.'

'I'm not your wife!' Her small, white teeth snapped. 'Not yet.'

Even her beautiful skin blanched in shock. 'You can't mean that,' she whispered.

'Oh I do!' The assurance came out as a caustic growl.

'This is madness!' She stared up into his gleaming eyes.

'Then we just have to accept it.' His chiselled mouth twisted. 'I want you, your heart, your mind, your body.' His gaze moved significantly over her satiny flesh.

'How could you bear to have me for a wife?' she challenged him. 'It wouldn't work. You know it. I know it.'

'You're always persecuting yourself.' He held her face with his hand. 'I won't see Jonathan between us. Only you.'

'Adrian . . .' She tried to stay him for an instant longer. 'The last thing Jonathan would have ever wanted was for me to love you.'

He was silent so long that she cried out in anguish. 'Don't you believe me?'

'There's a great deal I don't believe, but I believe that.' His voice was very quiet and she tensed beneath his hands.

'Jonathan lied to destroy me in your eyes. Why didn't he succeed? You know all about me, yet you still want me?'

His hands moved down over her curving bare shoulders. 'Is this the time when you are at most risk of becoming pregnant?'

'Would you take me if there was any danger?'

'I intend to take the greastest possible care of you, Kathryn. What's the answer?'

'The risk is small.' She flung her head to the side.

'So.' He bent his head.

She cried out his name in involuntary alarm, but then abruptly she felt the tremendous sexual pull arrowing through her body to its secret core. Her head pushed right back into the nest of cushions and her back arched as his tongue incited one nipple, then the other, into tight little peaks tingling with eroticism.

She felt the edge of his teeth, then his lips and she didn't realise that funny little keening sound that she could hear, was herself. It was a true measure of her feeling for him that even a little preliminary love-play could sear her entire body with heat.

'I want to undress you,' he told her urgently, his dominant face dark with intent. 'I can't stand *any* barrier.'

She was dizzy with desire, yet she neither helped nor hindered him, her skin glowing as though lit from within. He was holding her like a baby now, her lustrous head fallen forwards, her white breasts crushed against him. Deep tremors were running through her body and very gently he lowered her back against the bed where her magnolia body glowed against the rich, sombre background like an exquisite painting.

'It's never been like this. Never!' His hands stroked down over the slopes of her rose-peaked breasts to her silken thighs. 'Something very powerful brought us together, Kathryn. I felt it when we met.'

'But what name?'

Her voice was so shaken he bent his dark head and kissed her mouth hard. 'Karma. Kismet. Fate. You believe in it, don't you?'

'I believe in it,' she whispered poignantly, 'but how can I know how it will turn out?'

'Can't you trust me?' His voice had the caress of dark velvet.

'I trusted Jonathan when we met.'

Something primitive and elemental glittered in his eyes. 'Did Jonathan make flame burn along your veins? Did you move your legs so restlessly for him? I want to know everything about you, Kathryn. I'm going to know.'

His arms slid under her, gathering her up so she was compelled to respond to him with unprecedented abandon. The upper half of her body was afire with stimulation, but the lower was frustrated for the same excitation.

'Adrian!' She locked her slender arms behind his head and tried to pull him down to her.

'Slowly, Kathryn. I want to show you how it can be.'

It didn't seem possible she was so innocent of sensuality. She had been made love to many times. Made love to, or selfishly taken? There was a profound difference. She had never known such deep-mouthed kissing, such ravishment by a man's hands. It could not have been called tender, though his hands were ultra-sensitive. There was too much urgency for that. It was mind-bending, heart-expanding eroticism conducted by a master on an unmistakeably responsive body.

Her bra and slip made a shimmery pool on the carpeted floor but he made no attempt to remove her single remaining garment or caress her intimately. Every other inch of her body his hands and mouth had moved over and she was making small involuntary whimpering sounds as her frustration became too intense.

'Have you slept alone, Kathryn?' he challenged her, the tempest that was in him accentuating the taut mask of his chiselled features. 'Have you slept alone since you met me?'

She denied him an answer, drawing up one slender leg. 'You want me, Adrian, don't you?'

Now almost violently she was naked all over and admitting a lover's hand to the most sensitive, secret place of her body. The excitement was so intense it was shattering, and her body writhed as though racked.

'Yes I want you,' he told her harshly. 'Now I'm going to make you want me.'

Such an onslaught followed she was driven to digging her long nails into his back. She was shocked and magnetised by the sensuality he unlocked in her. 'Please!' she begged him for urgent release, but he only continued to prolong the exquisite torment.

'In time, Kathryn,' he promised gently, drawing away from her and gathering the long hair that flowed down her back. 'Such a mane of hair! A woman's glory.'

'Can't you help me?' Why had this one man the power to unleash her sexual longings? she thought frenziedly. He was handling her deliberately, evoking multiple wrenching sensations at will.

'I like you this way.'

Her body might never have been explored before. It was torture not to have him deep inside her. Her heart was beating like a triphammer, the flame that was in her, overheating her white skin. She was alight with desire. Whatever Jonathan had taught her was like the ripples at the edge of the sea compared to this rising, mighty surge. Her delicate nipples were tight and tingling from his ministrations and every muscle in her body was trembling in anticipation and response.

'Your skin is like satin,' he murmured, running his tongue along her soft, inner thigh.

'You're tormenting me. You know you are.' Her eyelids fluttered wildly and she tipped back her head, her softly throbbing mouth parting on a moan.

It was maddening ... maddening ... full of a fiery ecstasy.

'You want me to be part of you, don't you?'

Her eyes were tightly closed and she couldn't speak.

'Then why are you letting me love you?'

She was helpless to stop it, fast coming to the point of no control.

'What's happening to you, Kathryn. Tell me?' His head lowered to her breast and suddenly, terrifyingly, her orgasm, tightly budded, began unfolding like the petals of some marvellous grandiflora, spreading ... spreading ... opening out from her centre and filling her entire body right up to her throat.

'You want me now,' he muttered triumphantly, so

acutely tuned to her, he entered her deeply, his lean and powerful male form arched over her in the classic pose of possession. His own climax was thundering through his body and just as he bore down on her, she arched up to him in frantic rapturous response, such forces at work in them that Kathryn had the fearful sensation she might black out. Ecstasy was violent. So violent she could feel her consciousness dissolving and she struggled against it.

'Adrian!' Her brief, passionate cry was sharp and birdlike and even as she heard his deep answering groan the ascendancy passed swiftly from him to her as her body drained his of the life force. It was she who held him tightly, wrapped now, as they climaxed together, soaring . . . soaring . . . as fulfillment came roaring for them, lifting them free of earth's bounds.

They were in a new universe of rose-coloured plains where everything was very different, very beautiful and very strange. It even had a sun but it was exploding . . . exploding . . . shooting needles of fiery gold. Her heart threatened to burst out of its cage, just as excitement threatened to engulf her mind.

'Kathryn, you go beyond . . . anything!' His powerful body was shuddering in reaction and he covered her mouth voluptuously with his own. 'So much love . . . passion.'

Tears like diamond drops, slipped from her eyes.

They lay exhausted, body to body, nerves jumping and throbbing in an excitement that even now could not spend itself. Never before in her life had she felt so intensely. Not even when her beloved little Cam had been placed in her arms.

Their coming together had gone beyond anything. Just as she had known. She did not fully understand it, but she acknowledged it from the depths of her being. Through those long nights with Jonathan she had given pleasure and received little. Now she saw how it should be. With Adrian. The most exultant celebration even if she had gone to it with anguish in her heart.

'You wanted that, didn't you?' He gathered her to him, cradling her head on his shoulder. Her hair was damp all around her temples, causing little ringlets to spring around her face. 'I didn't hurt you?'

'No.' She felt as though she had come through a great storm and all that mattered now was survival. She was so spent that even her heart had slowed. Nothing in her experience had prepared her for this merging. Two beings as one. She was moon and he was night. It was an impossibly beautiful, long thrall.

'Kathryn?' His silvered eyes contemplated her suspended state of yearning, the submissive curve of her naked body. He saw that she had been crying, her long black lashes stuck together in spikes like a child's. 'Give up your grief, enchanted one. Haven't you a right to happiness?'

'Happiness is a word I've only heard about.' Her voice was no more than a soft flutter.

'You've known it tonight.' His hands moved to her breasts and suddenly, incredibly she was aroused again. How was that possible?

His mouth came down over hers and she submitted. He turned her quickly, his hand on her lower back pressing her ever closer to him.

He desired her again.

Her long slender legs quivered and twined through his, creating rippling sensations from the tips of her toes to the top of her head. Her thighs melted and she conjoined the sleek apex of her body with the hard press of his manhood.

Renewed excitement filled the air, and somewhere inside her, her faltering energy was replenished as if from an infintely deep pool.

'You make me insatiable!' he groaned, a primitive sound deep in his throat. 'You're that kind of woman.'

She could not withstand him, though his words flailed her naked flesh. For better or worse, did it matter? However much he wanted her and his strong body trembled in her arms, some part of him would continue to blame her for another man's destruction.

'Kathryn!' he cried, and she gave herself up to a dark fantasy.

# CHAPTER EIGHT

JUST as Adrian had foretold, the passionate wildness of that fateful night bound Kate more pwerfully to her unhappy past. Comparisons between Jonathan and his cousin were inevitable and terrible. Kate recognised her feelings of anguish were futile, but nevertheless, she could not prevent them. What she did do was withhold herself from Adrian and immerse herself in three major artwork projects that took up most of her time.

'I don't want to interfere, my dear,' Marcia told her, 'but you have a duty to your family and friends. You can't keep turning Gil away. I know you find your work satisfying, but fine young men like Gil Ralston aren't that easy to find. You'll remarry for certain, so it might as well be the right person.'

No one could be more right than Gil, so far as Marcia was concerned. His mother and father were among the Dowlings closest friends, and Gil was a very amenable young man, subject to his elders and thus unlikely to cause disruption to Marcia's future plans. Gil himself took exception to Kate's increasing unavailability, so in the end she had to tell him that although she found him a charming companion she was much too independent to consider a serious involvement with anyone.

'It was cruel, Kathryn, to lead him on,' Marcia said after she had heard the whole story from Gil's mother. 'He would have made a good husband and a kind, loving stepfather to my darling Cameron.'

'But I don't love him, Marcia,' Kate was moved to exclaim wearily. 'Besides, I've had enough of marriage to last me all my life.'

It was Charles who constrained Marcia not to hector a pressured Kate. 'She means well, Kate dear,' he spoke to Kate soothingly. 'My poor wife is terrified someone unsuitable is going to snatch you and our grandchild away. You've become very precious to us and Marcia has always felt Gil was one of the family. He's a good fellow, but not your type by a long way. I've tried to tell Marcia this, but she won't listen. She's very headstrong is my Marcia and she's too old to change her ways now.'

Even Adam's smiles were getting very thin. 'You're a changed girl, Katie,' he told her.

'Not at all, I'm the same person.'

'Someone's got to you while I wasn't looking. Bent your mind. I'd say it was Pender only he's always up to his neck in some *cause célèbre*.'

The one uncomplicated joy was Cam. Everyone adored him and for the weeks of Charles's convalescence, Kate was much too compassionate to even consider going ahead with her own plans. They had to be shelved but at least she had settled into the household more like a daughter than the strange in-law she had once felt herself to be. Marcia interfered constantly it was true, but it was equally certain she had Kate's well-being at heart.

'You're getting much too thin, my girl,' she told Kate one morning at breakfast, pinching her arm. 'You can get anorexia.'

'What's anorexia, Nanna?' Cam asked.

'Something you don't have to worry about, my little darling,' Marcia smiled at him warmly. 'Eat up your muesli.'

With his return to health, Charles had begun to pick up some of his business interests, and when he was able, he liked to discuss them with Adrian who, predictably, had a brilliant business brain. On these occasions Kate kept to the safety of her studio, but as she feared, Adrian was wont to invade her privacy any time he felt like it.

She was at her drawing board early one evening when Adrian knocked on the door.

'How timid you are, Kathryn,' he taunted her smoothly. 'Aren't you ever going to come out of hiding?'

'I suppose I should.' She put down her pen and arched her back. 'I've always been one to work obsessively.'

'I did hear that you told poor old Gil to stop bothering you.'

'Not at all.' She began to tidy up. 'I simply told him I had no wish for any serious commitment.'

'What a pity. He would have kept you very safe and protected.'

'So Marcia said.'

'Anyone but me,' he gave her a tight smile.

'You know it. I know it,' Kate returned in a brittle voice. 'None of us can make Jonathan go away.'

'Sorry—I can.'

'Marcia can't. I can't.'

'And both of you seem to consider it fair to punish me. Jonathan wasn't the only one who suffered by comparisons. I was a very observant child. I think I've recognised all my life Marcia resented me. It's sad when you think about it. She put a lot of pressure on Jonathan and me, but I don't think she'll ever face up to it.'

'Probably not,' Kate sighed, defeated. 'All I know is it would upset her dreadfully if I told her——'

'You loved me?'

'I don't love you, Adrian,' she cried emotionally. 'I'm mesmerised by you. My blood surges every time I lay eyes on you or when I hear your voice. It's like a sickness, a fever.'

'And that's not love?' He came to her and caught the point of her chin in hard, hurting fingers.

'Relationships don't begin and end in bed!' The hot blood mounted to her cheeks and her eyes glittered like gems.

'Are you sure, Kate?' he asked very suavely. 'You seem to find it very hard to admit that you're a very passionate woman. In fact you're one of those women it's impossible to think of without picturing you in bed.'

His eyes and his expression incited her to fury. 'I detest you!' she cried.

'Detest me all you like, but I'm getting you to myself tonight. You can't show me what making love to you is like, then lock yourself away.'

'Adrian—please.' She made a tremendous effort to break his grip. 'Someone might come in.'

His silver eyes appraised her with a flicker of contempt. 'You mean Marcia would hate seeing you in my arms. You belong there. Don't imagine for one moment you're fooling me, though I expected it would take weeks for you to dispense with the melodramatics.'

Her futile struggles were making her breath come in shaky gasps. 'Cam might come.'

'Cam is reading a junior version of *Treasure Island* to his grandfather.' He caught her arms and brought them together behind her back. 'I'm not hurting you, Kate.'

'You're killing me.' The tears leapt into her eyes.

'My poor darling, there's no need for all this agony,' he told her sombrely. 'Hasn't there been enough of it in the past? You remind me of a rose. A wild rose with the most beautiful, intoxicating perfume.'

'Don't, Adrian. I mean it.'

'Your voice is a whisper. I care nothing for what you say. Your body is trembling. It tells the truth.'

She felt two sensations almost simultaneously, the

exquisite stab of desire and the sudden yielding of her limbs.

'Kathryn.' He gathered her to him crushingly, the hunger that coursed through him finding relief in the plundering of her soft, open mouth. And he needed more. She was wearing a silk shirt with her cotton jeans and he plunged his hand through the deep V closing over her naked breast. She had not bothered to wear a bra and he must have known, because he had never taken his eyes off her.

Within seconds she was breathing very deeply. Her breasts were enormously responsive and it was no secret to him. It was, rather, a powerful stimulant to them both, so involuntarily she began to move against him.

'God!' he said thickly. 'Tell me now you don't want me.'

She could feel the arrow of excitement flaming through her body. If she let it it would reach her brain and she would forget everything. Every consideration . . . all natural caution.

'Come with me tonight. We need make no excuses. Why should we need to? Your life is your own.'

Whatever the pain, the recriminations, it was worth it. Sighing deeply she went to answer, but the door behind them flew open and Cam launched himself into the room.

'Were you hugging Mummy, Adan?' Cam asked with delighted interest.

'You can't have all that pleasure to yourself, little pal.' Adrian's training stood him in enormous stead because instantly he was warmly reassuring to the child.

'You might have knocked on the door, darling,' Kate pointed out gently. 'It's good manners.'

'Sorry, Mummy,' Cam looked up at her earnestly. 'I keep forgetting.'

'Did you finish your book?' Adrian asked him.

Cam gave him a wide grin. 'Grandpa said I gave it a whole new meaning. I'm a very good reader. What are you doing in here?' he asked. 'Nanna wants to know if Adan is staying for dinner.'

Marcia arrived at the studio door just as Cam was speaking. She always seemed afraid to leave Kate and Adrian on their own too long, now she was agitatedly twisting her fingers.

'I expect you have things to do, Adrian?'

'Oh, don't go, Adan!' Cam said wistfully.

Adrian moved over to the child and smoothed a hand over his silky curls. 'I don't know what to do now. I want to stay with you and I promised your mother I'd take her out to dinner.'

'Take Mummy,' Cam smiled broadly. 'Isn't that what you want?'

'As long as you're happy.'

'I am. I can call you up all the time.'

'He does too!' Adrian announced amusedly. 'Next time perhaps, Marcia. Thank you for asking.'

Kate was dressing in her room when Marcia called in on her.

'Don't you think this has gone far enough, Kathryn?' she asked tersely, closing the door and stepping further into the room.

'Forgive me, Marcia, I'm not sure what you mean.' Kate half turned away to clip an earring on her ear.

'My dear, you know I'm not happy seeing you and Adrian together.'

'Why is that, Marcia?' Kate asked, suddenly on edge.

'It's not suitable.'

'I don't know why you should say that.'

Marcia walked across to an armchair and slumped into it. 'I don't think I can imagine anything worse than you and Adrian together.'

'I think I understand, Marcia,' Kate said. 'It's difficult to look at him and not remember Jonathan.'

'Adrian is family.'

'Yes he is, but he's not my family,' Kate said with difficulty. 'There's no law man-made or natural that says I can't marry Adrian.'

'You'd do that?' Marcia looked up with tears in her eyes.

'Oh, please, Marcia, help me,' Kate implored. 'I'm hopelessly helplessly in love with him. It has nothing to do with Jonathan. The strong physical resemblance is there, it's true, but Adrian is a completely different man.'

'Of course. He was always different, even as a child,' Marcia fumbled for a handkerchief. 'Don't do this, Kathryn. I really care about Adrian. I do, but if he marries you, my little Cam will be gone forever. Lost to me almost as soon as you brought him into our lives.'

'But Marcia, how can you say that?' Kate went to her looking steadily into Marcia's eyes. 'Wasn't it Adrian who was instrumental in bringing us here? Isn't he a devoted nephew to Charles? You and Olivia are close friends. Both families are in and out of one another's homes frequently. Adrian is a deeply compassionate man. You hear him talk all the time. You know his views. He's an intensely caring person.'

'But he's his own man, isn't he, Kathryn? Master of his own home. He won't be satisfied being a step-father to Cameron. In no time at all he'll be his real father with all a father's rights. Cam will be brought up the way Adrian wants. He'll brook no interference, you can be certain of that.'

'I don't know what you're getting at, Marcia,' Kathryn said in some distress. 'Cam is my son. I've raised him so far and I think I've done a pretty good job of it. He's a good, sweet, beautiful boy.'

'Oh, he is, he is!' Marcia cried distractedly. 'But it's beginning again, don't you see? Jonathan idolised Adrian as a boy when a lot of the time he ignored his own mother. Cam is different, I know—Jonathan could be difficult even at Cam's age—but I'm frightened of losing him. I've got so used to his holding my hand!'

'Marcia, dear,' Kate went down on her knees before the older woman. 'Whatever happens, and I have not agreed to marry Adrian, I'll make sure Cam is never parted from his grandparents. I'm a believer in family. I think it of the greatest important that Cam should have the love and guidance of his grandparents.'

'Well I'll tell you it won't be easy with Adrian. He's not an easy, sweet person like dear Gil. Gil would have allowed me a lot of say in my grandchild's life. Adrian needs no one. He's so clever and confident and he'll expect Cam to be the same.'

'And why not?' Kate put her two hands over Marcia's. 'Cam is a very bright and confident little person. I think, Marcia, you and I are still suffering a few hang-ups over Jonathan. In a sense his tragedy has dominated our lives. There was an unhappy, dark side to Jonathan's nature, and when those moods were on him he did a lot of damage. Your view of Adrian has been distorted by Jonathan's reaction to being outshone by an older cousin. Should you blame Adrian endlessly because he happened to be born brilliant? In a way he was punished for it. Jonathan loved him, I know, but consciously or subconsciously he was pathologically jealous. Tell me one instance when Adrian has displayed a proprietorial attitude towards Cam? He's delighted to see him so fond of you, of his grandfather. There's nothing mean or even ordinary about Adrian. He does recognise your rights, Marcia.'

'I'm sorry I troubled you,' Marcia said bleakly. 'I

know all Adrian's good points. Kathryn. I've heard them unrolled in my ear for more than thirty years. If the truth be told, I'd be reluctant to see you marry *anyone* so soon ... but Adrian! In the first place he's too close and in the second, I mean what I say. Adrian will be master in his own home. Whatever becomes of my darling Cam it will reflect him!'

For the life of her Kate couldn't see that as a bad thing. Adrian was universally respected and admired. He was held to be a man of the highest integrity which obviously he had to be to have reached such eminence in his profession, but Marcia's response was almost entirely emotional. As indeed, Kate was forced to admit to herself, was her own. Both of them were haunted by Jonathan. Perhaps it might have been different had there not been the striking physical resemblance between the two cousins ... and the disparity of character. For all the rationalisation, Kate viewed Marcia's feelings with compassion.

They were scarcely clear of the house when Adrian attacked the problem. 'Marcia has upset you, hasn't she?'

'Forgive me, please, Adrian, but I can't talk about it.'

'You want me to say, all right, then let the matter pass? We have to talk, Kathryn.'

'It hurts me so much.'

'I can see you're tearing yourself to pieces. You've always been slender, now I scarcely dare to touch you, lest you break.'

'Can't you understand how Marcia feels?'

'My dear,' he said quietly, 'Marcia has no right to arrange your life to suit her plans. She was almost rushing you into a relationship with Gil. You know why, surely? Marcia is happiest when she can manipulate people.'

'I realise that.'

'So what is the tremendous problem?'

'God, this is crazy,' Kate burst out passionately, 'to fall in love with you. I wanted some peace in my blighted life.'

'Stop that,' he said firmly, 'you're talking absolute nonsense. I know it's all very sudden and I can't even attempt to explain it, but the fact is I want you and I'm never going to let you go. I intend to take the greatest possible care of you and Cam. I love you both. The trouble is, Kathryn, you haven't entirely broken away from the tragedy of your marriage. You know perfectly well in your heart and your mind that there'll be no repetition with me. You trust me. You know you do. You trust me to be a good father to Cam, but ghosts of the old emotions are causing you continuing pain. You're like the princess in the ivory tower running round and round with no form of escape. If you only sat down and thought about it, discussed it with me, you'd find that you really have the key. If what you tell me is true then it's obvious Jonathan did his best to manipulate your mind. Are you going to let it work or are you going to let go?'

'I'm so confused.' She bowed her head into her hands.

'Then let me free your mind of confusion. You love me. You need me. That's all that matters.'

'It seems to be when you say it like that.'

'Darling, you can hardly expect me to prevaricate. I'm not a ditherer. I've been waiting for you all my life and I believe you've been waiting for me. Destiny brought us together.'

'It could have done it earlier.'

'You have Cam. Would you deny him?'

'Never!' Her little indrawn breath was shocked. 'I can hear the voice of reason, Adrian, but it doesn't effectively clear my clouded emotions. Possibly had you been married you could appreciate more keenly what I'm feeling. Almost from the instant I met you, you wiped Jonathan out. Just like that. It's what he always worried about. I think he was terrified of our ever meeting. He tried to destroy me in your eyes by making up whatever story suited him at the time of writing. I did tell him I would leave him if he didn't seek help. He was so possessive he used to try to stop me from even leaving the flat, but I was never unfaithful to him. It simply didn't occur to me. If only you know how it was! I was brought up to believe marriage was forever, not a short period of living together and a handshake at the end. Whereas . . .'

'Kathryn,' Adrian reached out and put his hand over hers, 'I understand completely what you're trying to tell me, and I don't want you upsetting yourself any further. I think you've had to drive yourself too hard. When other girls were enjoying a carefree youth, you obviously had lots of problems. You've done a wonderful job of rearing Cam and you're successful in your own right, but I suspect you've been burning up your energies too fast. Charles tells me you work until all hours.'

'I work best at night. It's not work anyway.'

'You mightn't' see it that way because you're naturally gifted, but it's work all the same—just sitting at the drawing board for long hours. You continually have to come up with fresh material. By the way, I'd like you to meet Paul Leighton. I acted for him once when he was being harrassed by some crank who objected to his portrait of the P.M.'

'I remember that,' Kate turned to him in surprise.

'You should, it went national. Anyway, Paul and I have been friendly ever since. I've spoken to him about you—your ability. I've even shown him that beautiful pastel drawing you did of Cam for my mother. He was impressed. He understands exactly how you've been preoccupied with becoming a commercial success, but he said he'd be happy to allow you to work with him for a while. I'm sure you'll agree he could help you enormously. His forte is portraiture and it seems certain you have that gift.'

Within moments Kate's mood shifted to being almost exultant. 'You mean he'd be prepared to allow me to work with him? But that's an incredible honour. I really don't feel worthy.'

'Well much as he's grateful for what I was able to do for him, I'm certain he wouldn't take you on unless he thought you had real talent. Oddly enough he said his wife and daughters had lots of your cards "cluttering up the place". It appears they love them. He is, of course, famous these days, but he was just a struggling young artist for many years. I spoke to him about you, but he made the decision entirely on his own initiative.'

Kate's face which had a uniquely sweet expression, was a study in delight. 'I've wondered all my life if I could be really good. I had my dreams.'

'And there's no reason why you shouldn't be given the opportunity to make them come true. If I hadn't been glancing through some greetings' cards at random I would never have spotted the family face. Your gift is such I knew that face immediately. The rest we know. Beautiful as your cards are, they escape sentimentality. Paul said as much. He's a touch eccentric as you might appreciate, but I'm sure you'll get on well. I'll even hazard a guess he'll want to paint you. You have the most incredibly beautiful skin and striking colouring.' He glanced at her and smiled gently. 'Feeling better?'

'I simply don't know what to say. You're too full of surprises.'

'I'll try to keep them always as pleasant. By the way, I thought Cam might have my collection of British soldiers with the fort.'

'Surely they're Edwardian toys?' Kate asked.

'I had them at his age and I certainly knew how to look after them. I'm sure Cam will too. It's good to begin early on in life, to learn how to look after things.'

'You look exquisite!' Adam told her when they met next day for lunch. 'I never thought a blue eyed girl could wear jade.'

'Incredibly it works.' Kate shifted the small central vase of flowers a little to the left. 'Gosh, I'm hungry: What about Crab Louis with cucumber?'

'Why not?' Adam returned cheerfully. 'You're shouting aren't you?'

'I wish you would allow me for once.'

'Having lunch with you, Kate, in the highlight of my day. How's the fashion project going?'

'I haven't had word. Too early perhaps. Stylistic impressions for an after-five boutique. Olivia loved them. She thought them very beautiful and romantic. I think they're ideal for the purpose. They'll adorn invitations to private showings and parades, associated advertising, the logo on the salon's elegant carry bags and boxes. That kind of thing, but what really has me excited is the opportunity to work with Paul Leighton.'

'Paul Leighton?' Adam frowned. 'That rings a bell.'

'The famous painter, dear boy.' Kate's glowing eyes were the colour of turquoise.

'But in what capacity?' Adam asked, obviously at sea.

'I'm going to sit, stand, kneel at his feet. I'm going to watch him while he works. He's going to watch me. I'm going to have the benefit of his enormous skill, his artistic approach. In short I'm going to learn how to paint!'

'That's lovely, dear. But what for?'

'Adam—do you know what you're saying?'

'Aren't you doing well enough as you are?'

'I've never done anything real!'

Adam drew back his lips in a wry grimace. 'You're making more money than I am.'

'I know and it's fun too, but this is a wonderful opportunity for me, Adam. I've always had ambitions, you know.'

'And you've done a great deal,' Adam pointed out. 'Has Pender arranged this? Is that it?'

Kate sat back in her chair, staring into Adam's faintly scowling face. 'As a matter of fact he did.'

'My God, he's clever.'

'I don't know what you mean.'

'Of course you've spoken to him about it.'

'No.'

'He knew somehow,' Adam maintained. 'It's the one bloody thing I would never have thought of and I got you started.'

'Believe me, Adam, I'm deeply grateful for all that you've done.' Kate's early euphoria was quickly fading away. 'It's simply that Adrian is the sort of person who works at his full potential and he's attempting to help me.'

'Surely you've got enough on your hands,' Adam asked almost sharply. 'Lunch is all we've been able to manage in over a week. I came here, Katie, to be with you. Now I have the feeling I don't mean much to you anymore.'

'You can't mean that, Adam,' Kate said faintly.

'I do. I even thought there was a chance you would come to your senses and marry me.'

'Oh, Adam!'

'It can't be unexpected surely. I've loved you as long as I've known you. I had to stand aside and watch you marry a man who tried to keep you in bondage. The whole period was one long nightmare. I think I nearly went out of my mind.'

'But you always acted so calm and reasonable.'

'My dear, I was forced to. In my opinion your dear Jonathan was dangerous. My greatest fear was that he would hurt you.'

'Don't let's talk about those days, Adam,' Kate begged him. 'You know how much I value our friendship.'

'Will you marry me?'

'I can't, Adam. I can't.'

'Yes, but you'd marry Pender, wouldn't you?'

Kate's blue eyes blazed. 'Listen, Adam, I haven't said I'd marry anyone.'

'Of course. You're terrified. I could cry for you, darling.'

'I don't think I want lunch after all,' Kate murmured quietly and reached for her handbag.

'You must have thought it yourself, dear.' Adam persisted. 'It's not so strange. Jonathan gave you a very bad time. It's just as they say; once bitten, twice shy.'

'Could anyone blame me?' Her eyes shimmery, Kate went to rise.

'That's it, Kate, run away. You don't want to talk about Pender. You're in love with him. I'm not a complete fool. I've seen you together. But what a little fool! You've gone and fallen in love with the one man who couldn't possibly make you happy. It would be just like you never left Jonathan.'

'No!' Kate cried out in ringing denial. 'If you believe that, you never knew the first thing about either of them.'

'Please wait, Kate, please!' Hurt and upset Adam made a last effort to detain her.

'I came here to have lunch with one of my dearest, oldest friends only that friend has gone away.'

'Katie, try to calm yourself.' Adam held her arm.

'I am calm, Adam.' Kate removed his hand with

surprising strength. 'The last thing I have ever wanted was to hurt you. I've always been very honest.'

'If you insist on going, I'll go with you.'

'No, I must run. Call me if you want to. I'll always be your friend.'

It came as a further unpleasant shock to Kate to have her freelance fashion commission rejected only a day later. To make it worse, there was little apology and no explanation.

Charles was all business. 'My dear, they haven't even returned your portfolio. I'd get it back as soon as possible. You didn't sign anything to the effect they could retain the drawings even if they weren't used?'

'Not at all!' Kate felt disappointed and drained. 'I really don't understand it. I understood the owner very much liked my work. Marcia thought them very romantic and there isn't a more beautiful or glamorous woman than Olivia. Both of them gave me the O.K.'

'You're entitled to a better explanation than that,' Charles confirmed bluntly.

In the next hour Kate made two 'phone calls to the salon and was plainly fobbed off.

'Adrian will tell you your legal position in an instant,' Charles advised. 'The first rule in business is to know the people you're dealing with. You do read everything before you sign any contract?'

'I do,' Kate assured him. 'Ah well, I suppose I can't sell all my work.'

'If you don't sell,' Charles said briskly, 'you want to know why.'

Kate moved to the open window of Charles' study and looked out. 'Such a beautiful day!'

'Perfect!' Charles gave a deep sigh, resounding with satisfaction. 'I've never been so happy in my life. Never!'

'I'm so glad.' Kate turned to look into his eyes. 'I've wanted to speak to you about something.'

'I know, dearest Kathryn. You want—need—your own home?'

Suddenly she laughed at the peaceful expression on his face. 'You know we're all going to remain very close.'

'I trust you implicitly, my dear.'

'That's good to know. No, Charles, it's something else.' She moved backwards and sat down opposite the desk. 'Adrian has asked me to marry him.'

Although it wasn't a complete surprise, Charles bounded up. 'My dear, are you telling me there's going to be a celebration?'

'Could it really be a celebration, Grandfather?' Kate asked. 'I can see you're happy, but Marcia feels differently.'

'Marcia will come around,' Charles promised. He bent his head and kissed Kate's cheek. 'You paid a high price for marrying my son. Nothing ever happened in the way we intended. I loved my son deeply, but I was always aware of his introvert nature, and I have punished myself because I thought I had failed him as a father. When I go back in time I see him as a little boy. We had some wonderful times, all of us. Jonathan used to get into such mischief and Adrian was always scolded by Marcia because he was older and far stronger, in every way. Of course I recognised it was Jonathan's way of trying to get attention. When the gods handed out gifts they showered them on Adrian and Jonathan was always furious he had to walk in Adrian's shadow. It wasn't the ideal situation for either boy, but they were fantastically close. Close enough to be twins. The real trouble didn't start until Adrian embarked on his remarkable career. Jonathan admired him so much. He always tried to be like him. When he realised he couldn't be, he came to believe it was the ultimate humiliation. He never ever tried to develop his own strengths. He just gave up.' Kate leaned close to him and Charles put his arm around her shoulder. 'You love Adrian, don't you, Kathryn?'

'Yes, and it shocks me.'

'Because he's so extraordinarily like Jonathan physically?'

Kate shook her head. 'Worse than that. I can't carry a picture of Jonathan at all.'

'And you feel sad and guilty?'

'Yes.' Kate dipped her head. 'Jonathan wrote Adrian a series of letters about his unhappy marriage. He made lots of charges that simply weren't true. He wrote many things about me. On the other hand, he often told me about his relationship with Adrian. I was never sure if he loved him or hated him, but it was obvious Adrian played a significant role in Jonathan's life. Jonathan would have thought it the ultimate defeat to lose me to his cousin.'

'Dearest Kathryn,' Charles pointed out quietly, 'Jonathan is dead. You must let him go.'

'And you think Adrian and I could live together happily?'

Charles took her hands and held on to them. 'I would say Adrian has all the qualities to make you a wonderful husband and aren't you very glad he and Cam share such a deep bond? Cam accepted him on sight. All perfectly natural. They're family. As for you, I knew almost from the beginning Adrian had found the one woman he wanted. Every time he looked at you there was confirmation in his eyes. I think you'll find even Marcia was aware of a deep and immediate attraction.'

'Only it upsets her terribly.'

'I suppose you could marry Gil?' Charles suggested.

Kate looked up at him quickly, only to see the teasing light in his eyes. 'You think I'm being ultra-sensitive?'

'I'm sure of it, my dear,' Charles confirmed. 'Leave Marcia to me.'

# CHAPTER NINE

KATE'S rejected portfolio still didn't arrive so she decided to call in on Adrian after checking once more with the salon. The woman she had spoken to had expressed apologies, but sounded very vague when pressed for details. Mrs Doyle was out of town. Perhaps she could ring again. Kate felt she was being given the run-around and even Marcia advised her to speak to Adrian about the matter.

'What's the use of having a lawyer in the family if you can't get some free advice?'

'I never knew Adan was a lawyer,' Cam said. 'I thought he was a barrister?'

Marcia reached down and patted his head. 'Lawyer is an American term, my darling, but everyone seems to use it these days. Solicitors, barristers, they're lawyers.'

'I want to be a High Court judge.'

Marcia peered down at her little grandson with a funny look. 'You never said that before.'

'I'm going to defend people like Adan. I'm going to be strong and good.'

'Seriously, old chap,' Charles grasped his grandson's hand 'what about a spot of cricket?'

'Oh, goodie!' Cam cried. 'I expect you want to bat first.'

Kate waited until after lunch before she drove into the city. The day was very hot and sultry with an afternoon thunderstorm threatening. Marcia and Charles intended to take a quick run out to the beach to allow Cam to swim and Kate thought gratefully how an intensive swimming programme was working wonders in strengthening Cam's lungs and building up his physique. His resistance to infection was also stronger since he had turned into a water baby and she thought much of it wouldn't have been possible without all the extra supervision. It was a tribute to everyone's love that they all worked so hard at building Cam up. His last wheezing bout had been remarkably short.

All the leading barristers were housed together and as Kate stepped out of the lift and turned to walk along the corridor to Adrian's rooms, Adrian himself suddenly appeared at the far end accompanied by a petite blonde in black and white. Kate saw that she didn't even come up to his shoulder. Even at a distance it was obvious they were deep in a continuing conversation and their expressions were formally serious.

It was impossible to retreat and Kate decided she didn't really want to. Whatever Davina Adams was to Adrian, she had to know.

As she drew near the tap-tap of her high heels didn't even reach them. Whatever they were talking about, both of them were violently engrossed. Adrian's stunning profile was outlined against the warm dark gold of the window. He's everything to me, Kate thought. Whatever course she chose to take her life would never be the same again. But what is love? she thought sadly. Ecstasy, anger, the pain of disillusionment. Davina Adams was here with him now and Davina had loved him all her life.

Adrian was the first to see her, turning in her direction, his eyes like diamonds in his tanned face.

This is it, Kate thought. Tell me a story ... there's nothing easier.

'If it isn't dear Kathryn now!' Davina called out in a hard voice. Her green eyes were glassily bright and she held her slight body very tight.

'I'm sorry. Am I interrupting?' Kate sounded totally self-composed.

'Let's face it, Kathryn,' Davina said attackingly, 'you've been working hard on it ever since you arrived.'

'I'm serious, Davina, about what I just said,' Adrian declared with a hard edge to his voice.

'Oh, I believe you, darling!' Davina flared viciously. 'Anyone who crosses you is bound to get hurt.'

Kate suddenly hated the whole situation. She hated Davina. She hated herself. Adrian was diabolically clever.

'Kathryn.' As though reading every thought that sprang into her mind, Adrian suddenly caught her arm. 'Come in, won't you? Davina was just leaving.'

'Fine!' There was an extra flush on Davina's cheeks. 'Adrian and I have broken at last. It was lovely while it lasted.' She laughed again and looked at Kate. 'Good luck, my dear. You're going to need it.'

'I'm sorry, Davina,' Kate was suddenly moved to pity.

'You will be,' Davina warned. 'You couldn't handle one. How could you possibly handle the other?'

Before either of them could respond, Davina turned on her heel and rushed off.

'Come in, Kathryn,' Adrian said and Kate forced herself to walk through the door.

Bookcases lined the whole of one wall, gold print standing out clearly against dark leather bindings. It was almost like a small library, very masculine, comfortable and, now the door was shut, escape-proof.

'What are we supposed to do now?' she asked wryly and tossed her hair back from her face.

'We can always have a cup of coffee.' In fact he put two cups under the tap of a coffee machine.

'I had no idea Davina would be here.'

'She was here professionally.'

'That sounds exactly right,' Kate returned coolly.

He set a cup of coffee down on a small table beside her and moved back to lean against the massive, antique desk. 'Are you going to listen?'

'I only just walked in.'

'It's confusing, I know, Kathryn, but not at all what you're thinking.'

'Whatever it is I can face it.' Kate looked matter-of-factly at her slender crossed legs. She had worn a new, white dress, pleated, beautifully simple. She was just another crazy woman in love.

'You look beautiful,' he said, his voice deep and calm.

'When does a man accept one woman?'

'I think, my love, you want to find a weakness in me. An unconscious wish to banish me from your life.'

'Not too bad a guess.' It was a considerable effort to talk coolly when he was looking at her with a mixture of mockery and admiration.

'I don't think you understand. I'll never let you go. I know you better than you know yourself. You're the most loving, giving, vulnerable creature. You throw up defences on all sides, but I'm going to ignore them until they go away. You say one thing and feel another. You're going to taunt me very coolly when the tears are just behind your eyes.'

'So you've noticed?' She sprang up and walked to a tall bookcase, running her finger over the spine of a weighty legal volume. 'Surely one lifetime wouldn't be enough to get through this?'

'Not for me.'

'No.'

'Why can't you trust me?' he asked.

'You're right. Why can't I?' Emotion was enveloping her, showing in her flushed cheeks and dazzling blue eyes.

'When we've shared the most perfect, powerful, transforming loving?'

'I thought we had,' she said poignantly, 'but what's real?'

'What we've got.' He stopped her restless prowling by coming behind her and encircling her slender body, his arm crossed beneath her breasts. 'I don't think I want you bone-thin.' He hugged her closer dipping his head and brushing his mouth along her high cheekbones. 'You're fading away in my arms.'

It was impossible not to let her head fall back so he found the corner of her mouth. 'Don't you ever think there's a good reason for it.'

'You're terrified of surrendering up your love and trust.' Unhurriedly he slipped the single hook that caught the cross-over bodice of her dress. 'You've been punishing yourself relentlessly, but I won't allow it any more. This has gone too far. You know how your body reacts to mine. Why don't you trust it?' He slipped his hand over the high firm contour of her breast sheafed in almond lace. 'This is communication at its most elemental but isn't that central to passionate love between a man and woman.'

Her nipples were pinpoints of sensation. 'Adrian!' She moved back weakly against him.

'If only I could make love to you now!' He was already turning her into his arms.

'Well you can't.' Her breath was a scented mist.

'I think I can manage to kiss you, though.'

'And everything will turn out all right.'

'Not all men are bastards, my darling.' His mouth touched hers very gently and she moaned as the tip of his tongue entered her mouth through her open lips. Her heart fluttered voluptuously and he gathered her into him, his kiss deepening and deepening until her head was spiralling and every nerve in her body was twisting with desire.

How heated her skin became like hot satin and his
fingers caressed the arch of her long neck, the delicate
ridge of her collarbone and slid into the open neck of
her dress.

'Not here, Adrian!' Desperately she pulled her
mouth away.

'No, not here.' His voice was faintly slurred,
frustrated. It was impossible to doubt his ardour, the
length of her slender body pressed against his.

Even then she lifted her arms and laced them
around his neck. 'When there's only the two of us, I
feel infinitely secure.'

'Do you?' He leaned down and kissed her beautiful
mouth. 'I treasure that, Kathryn. Very much.' His
silver eyes were trained on her face, searchingly. 'You
said that like an exhausted child.'

'I do feel . . . vulnerable. It hurts me to say it, but
I've never loved a man, like this, before. I fell in love
with Jonathan, but Jonathan became a different
person. It was an unbearable situation.'

'And you told him you had to leave?'

'I had to.' Her blue eyes were huge and glistening.
'I felt I couldn't cope and I tried. There were times
when Jonathan was filled with a peculiar violence. I
guess I was afraid. I never told Jonathan about Cam.
He only wanted the two of us,' she gave a broken little
laugh. 'The two of us. It was all so terribly sad.'

'You should have had family. Most of all you should
have had me.'

'Have you any idea how bad that might have been?'

His silver eyes were startlingly brilliant. 'I would
have known how to protect you. Perhaps the very best
things come after struggle. I wanted you on sight, but
I don't have you, even yet. There's some inner cell of
you I have yet to reach.'

She shook her head and dropped her arms. 'You
know I've quite forgotten why I came here. Nothing

in this world seems serious when you start to make love to me.'

He caught her fingers and settled her in a chair. 'So—you saw Davina leave?'

'I did.' She stroked her temple with her fingers.

'And this doesn't suggest anything to you?'

'Nothing other than she's madly in love with you and tired of a go-nowhere situation.'

He gave a brief laugh. 'I know it's very ungallant of me, but my involvement with Davina was very short and over four or more years ago. Of necessity I see her all the time. We move in the same circles, but it would be quite idiotic to say I've been leading the dear girl on. She has an enormous capacity for self-deception. Women like Davina are always plotting something or other as well. When Charles mentioned to me the Zara Doyle thing I had a hunch Davina had something to do with it. Or rather it was Harry's doing for his precious girl. Davina might have been a different woman if her father hadn't spoiled her so outrageously.'

Kate just stared at him. 'You mean Harry Adams somehow influenced Mrs Doyle's decision?'

'Harry Adams and a couple of partners own the Chandler Building. Zara Doyle was very lucky to get her lease. I daresay Harry could squeeze her out if he wanted to. He's absolutely ruthless when he wants to be.'

'But how extraordinary!'

'Of course I wasn't sure but I've had a lot of training getting more out of people than they intend to say. From a flat denial, Davina finally admitted it all. To put it bluntly, she's always had it in for you.'

'Dear God!' Kate sighed. 'The lengths people will go to. Well, rather than have Mrs Doyle harassed in any way, we'll just drop it. I want my portfolio back, though.'

'You'll get it,' Adrian assured her. 'In fact it will be delivered by special courier to my rooms. Had Zara Doyle acted with more consideration for you I would have given her a bit of gratuitous advice, but as it is I don't feel so inclined.'

'Davina planned the whole thing?'

'Yes, Kathryn,' Adrian told her gently. 'Now, if you can't find any other way to thank me, what about if we have dinner at home tonight? I know an excellent catering service and I think we can just about manage to serve ourselves.'

'Adrian . . .' It was a whisper of protest with her heart in her eyes.

'Is that a yes?' He leaned down and tilted her chin.

'Yes.' She took a little shuddery breath and smiled back. 'Clearly you're a man who always gets his way.'

Things seemed to move very swiftly after that. No engagement was announced though Adrian gave Kate the most exquisite ring she could ever have wished for. He must have believed she had once owned another engagement ring of sapphires and diamonds, for the central stone in his ring was a magnificent ruby, its flawless deep crimson tinged with rose.

'My rose!' he told her and crushed her soft mouth.

The general reaction was of surprise and pleasure. All were in agreement it was time for Adrian to surrender his bachelor status, and if acute disappointment was experienced in certain households, the Dowlings and the Penders presented a delighted front to the world. Kate was certain, however, that deep within, Marcia was shedding a few tears. She kissed Adrian and congratulated him, but underneath the resignation were unhealed wounds.

Cam was ecstatic. Outside his mother, even Marcia and Charles had to concede, Adrian was his favourite person and now, joy of joys, Adrian was to be his father.

'It's super, Grandpa, isn't it?' he demanded of Charles.

'It is. It is,' Charles responded warmly with a hug. 'We'll have to make sure Adrian buys a house very close. We don't want to miss our boy.'

'You won't miss me, Grandpa,' Cam told his grandfather kindly. 'I'll always come over. Anyway Nanna told me this was going to be my house when I grow up.'

'Is that so?' Charles said with an amused quirk to his brows. 'Well you'll have to work hard and be successful so you'll be able to hold on to it.'

'Oh, I will, Grandpa,' Cam assured him. 'Mummy talks to me about being responsible.'

Cam was growing up.

Adam, when Kate told him, dropped all his hostile feelings at once. 'I always knew in my heart I wasn't the right man for you. Be happy, Kate. Knowing you has been the nicest part of my life.'

'Why don't we all go out on Sunday?' Charles suggested one morning. 'Have a picnic in some glorious spot? Cam loves us all around him.'

'Fine with me,' Adrian confirmed when Kate checked with him later. 'I know what Uncle Charles is up to. He's trying to effect a family reconciliation.'

'Why don't we ask Aunt Olivia to come?' Cam piped up with his suggestion.

'Then we'd have to take two cars,' Marcia pointed out. 'I'll tell you what—Aunt Olivia and I will take you to the beach one day next week, and if you're an especially good boy Grandpa will drive the Rolls.'

In the end Charles decided he wanted to be chauffeur driven so Adrian took the wheel. It was a brilliant day all blue and golden and they headed for a mountain resort area. The views as they were climbing became increasingly spectacular and the scents of the pine forests had them winding down the windows to breath in the wonderfully clean, aromatic air.

Members of the artists' colony had built the most spectacular timber houses clinging to the cliffs and Kate thought how marvellous it would be to wake up each morning to such phenomenal uninterrupted views of valleys and the surrounding mountains.

'It would be nice to have a weekend-cottage up here,' Adrian commented, rather seriously and Kate gave him a searching glance.

'You do need relaxation. But surely such difficult sites would make it very expensive?'

'I'll check it out.' Briefly he touched her hand. 'Basically they're very simple constructions.'

Food in the open air always tastes twice as delicious and Marcia had gone to a great deal of trouble preparing and packing a portable feast. There were cheeses and fruits, freshly baked rolls, salad greens in foil, lush tomatoes, a screwtop jar of dressing, chilled butter curls, a mountain of cold roast chicken, hard boiled eggs, a bowl of black olives, plump pastry pillows of pork and apple and turkey and cranberry and a huge glazed apple flan to have with the thermos of coffee.

'This is the life!' Charles rested back on the blue and white cushions contentedly. 'You've done a wonderful job, my dear. I can't think why we don't get out more often.'

It was all extraordinarily peaceful and afterwards, as Kate and Adrian volunteered to clear away, Marcia took Cam for a short walk.

'Hold on to Nanna's hand, darling,' Kate called. They were on a wide plateau and it was all perfectly safe, but with small children one had to be doubly cautious. Not that Cam was a disobedient child—far from it—but today was an exciting time for him.

Presentiments of danger are strange. One moment

Kate was packing plates into the hamper, and the next she was on her feet staring in the direction Marcia had taken.

'What is it, darling?' Adrian was instantly alerted.

'Why, nothing—I don't know.' Yet tentacles of apprehension clutched around her heart.

'I'll stroll down after them, shall I?'

'What is it, Kathryn?' Charles called, taking his head out of a book he had brought with him.

'Nothing,' Kate said weakly, but Adrian who was studying her saw a terrible anxiety in her face. He leaned over and very gently kissed her. 'I'll go and catch them up. I expect they're quite enjoying themselves.'

'Yes, Adrian. Please go.' Kate found that her hand was shaking. She had always been anxious about Cam and Olivia explained it to her once as 'the only child syndrome', but she had never experienced this inexplicable fright before. On that perfect day it was quite bizarre.

Adrian turned to go and Kate had the urgent feeling she should go with him quickly. In fact she did cry out, but her words were unintelligible as a woman's anguished cry echoed violently across the plateau and the deep valley below.

This is the end, Kate thought.

Adrian began running, covering the downward slope with fantastic speed. Charles was on his feet crying, 'Dear God!' Only then did Kate break out of her paralysis and race after Adrian, dashing her ankle against a rock in her headlong flight. Usually so fleet of foot, terror was making her indescribably clumsy and there were flashing lights before her eyes. The thing that she dreaded, what every parent dreaded, was pounding on her heart. Adrian had disappeared and as Kate cleared the slope looking down the lush dark green bank she faltered in stark horror and had to fight to retain consciousness.

Marcia was standing near the cliff's edge, two hands to her mouth and Adrian was lying near the extreme edge, head and shoulders bent downwards.

'Keep going, Kate.' A voice said to her in a calm detached way. 'Keep going.' She thought it was her grandmother. Someone else was sobbing and she realised she had her mouth open.

'Kathryn! Keep back.' Marcia cried out convulsively. 'Cameron . . . the edge gave way.'

Down in the valley someone was flying a kite. No ordinary kite, but a magical creation from a Chinese festival.

She dropped to the grass a few feet from Adrian and edged her way to him, her mental agony so extreme it was beginning to have a narcotic effect.

Adrian looked back, then carefully hauled her alongside. 'He's on a wide, flat ledge. I can get down, but I'll need help getting him up. You'll have to drive the car down here and get the tow rope from the trunk. I'll fasten it around us and the car will pull us up.'

'Is he conscious?' Kate's skin shone with a frightening pallor. She went to move forward and Adrian's grip on her tightened to bruising strength.

'Don't go any further. Cam's conscious and he's waiting for me to come to him.'

'How?' Kate was desperate to go after her son.

'You just leave it to me,' Adrian said with harsh decisiveness. 'It would be madness for you to attempt it. I'm an experienced climber.'

'Adrian—you could be killed. Cam is my son.'

'Well he just waved to me,' Adrian announced. 'Things like that simply take your breath away.'

'Adrian, it's me.' It was Charles's voice.

Adrian looked back over his shoulder. 'Listen, Charles, I've told Kate what to do. Cam is safe, but I have to get down to him.'

'He broke away from me—it was the kite, you see.' Marcia was sobbing terribly.

'The rope!' Charles cried urgently.

'Go, Kate!' Adrian said in a very hard, business-like voice. 'I won't make any mistakes.'

She ran all the way, leaping over rocks, insensible to the pain in her ankle. It was the most tremendous thing she had ever done, surrendering the responsibility for her child's life to another human being. She was scarcely aware this was the greatest trust of all, her mind given over to scrupulously obeying Adrian's instructions. He had every advantage over her. He was a strong man, superbly fit and a keen athlete. Hadn't she seen a showcase of college and University prizes?

The Rolls ate up the slope, its legendary suspension sailing over the bad patches. Charles ran to her and took the rope, flinging one end over the cliff face and securing the other to the big, powerful car's bumper bar.

'Put her in reverse, Kate, when I signal.'

If anything happens to them now, Kate thought, I might just drive right over.

Marcia had slumped to the grass like a woman in acute pain, but no one could go to her.

Charles lifted his arm and Kate shifted the transmission into reverse moving the big car slowly, smoothly, powerfully back towards the narrow path while the engine kept up a deep, steady thrum that eventually turned to a dull roar. She felt the wall of the left rear tyre scrape against a rock and as she groaned aloud in anguish Adrian's dark head appeared, then his shoulders, Cam clinging to him like a koala and she shouted aloud, 'Thank God!'

Afterwards they lay in the thick grass with Cam wedged between them.

'You were splendid, my boy!' Charles said with

enormous precision because his throat muscles weren't working properly. 'You deserve a medal.'

'Don't talk about it.' Adrian put out his arm and drew Kate and her little son closely to him.

Marcia sat holding her head with her husband's arm around her and away down in the beautiful green valley the coiling creature that was the Chinese kite continued to soar on the thermal currents. 'I'll never forget this day. Never!' Marcia cried convulsively. 'It will stay in my memory forever.'

'Except that it was a miracle, my dear,' her husband told her quietly. 'Cam was saved, and it was Adrian who saved him. Who could forget that?'

Hideously frightening though the experience had been, there was an intense closeness between them going home in the car.

Cam kept to the comfort of his mother's arms, but curiously, child-like, his shock trauma was already half erased. He even giggled once at being towed up by the Rolls and remembered to apologise to everyone for the great upset he had caused them.

'It was the kite,' he told them as though that explained everything. 'I saw one just like it on a poster. I think I could make a good one if I tried and coloured it in.'

Marcia moaned and looked out the window and Kate reached over and grasped her hand. It was a compassionate gesture and one that affected Marcia powerfully.

'When I calm down,' she said emotionally, 'I'll know this is the beginning of a new life. Let there be peace and love between us forever more!'

'Amen,' Adrian said. He glanced at Kate and was electrified to see her blue eyes filled with a wonderful radiance.

'I love you,' she said clearly.

'I love you too, Adan.' Cam lifted his curly head then dropped it back heavily on his mother's breast.

Marcia wiped a tear from her cheek and as Charles leaned towards her, he saw that she was smiling.

Life recovered and resumed and through the open windows of the car came the scent of the pines, clean and sweet.

# Harlequin Romance

## Coming Next Month

Available in September wherever paperback books are sold, or through Harlequin Reader Service.

In the U.S.
P.O. Box 1397
Buffalo, N.Y.
14240-1397

In Canada
P.O. Box 2800, Postal Station A
5170 Yonge Street
Willowdale, Ontario M2N 6J3

# Take 4 books & a surprise gift FREE

---

## SPECIAL LIMITED-TIME OFFER

---

Mail to    **Harlequin Reader Service®**

| In the U.S. | In Canada |
|---|---|
| 901 Fuhrmann Blvd. | P.O. Box 2800, Station "A" |
| P.O. Box 1394 | 5170 Yonge Street |
| Buffalo, N.Y. 14240-1394 | Willowdale, Ontario M2N 6J3 |

**YES!** Please send me 4 free Harlequin Presents® novels and my free surprise gift. Then send me 8 brand-new novels every month as they come off the presses. Bill me at the low price of $1.75 each ($1.95 in Canada)—a 11% saving off the retail price. There are no shipping, handling or other hidden costs. There is no minimum number of books I must purchase. I can always return a shipment and cancel at any time. Even if I never buy another book from Harlequin, the 4 free novels and the surprise gift are mine to keep forever.

116-BPR-BP6F

---

Name            (PLEASE PRINT)

---

Address            Apt. No.

---

City         State/Prov.        Zip/Postal Code

This offer is limited to one order per household and not valid to present subscribers. Price is subject to change.      DOP-SUB-1R

# ATTRACTIVE, SPACE SAVING BOOK RACK

Display your most prized novels on this handsome and sturdy book rack. The hand-rubbed walnut finish will blend into your library decor with quiet elegance, providing a practical organizer for your favorite hard-or soft-covered books.

**Only $9.95**

**Approximately 16" x 8" when assembled**

**Assembles in seconds!**

----------------------------------------

To order, rush your name, address and zip code, along with a check or money order for $10.70 ($9.95 plus 75¢ postage and handling) (New York residents add appropriate sales tax), payable to *Harlequin Reader Service* to:

In the U.S.

Harlequin Reader Service
Book Rack Offer
901 Fuhrmann Blvd.
P.O. Box 1325
Buffalo, NY 14269-1325

*Offer not available in Canada.*

BKR-1

# HARLEQUIN HISTORICAL

Explore love with Harlequin in the Middle
Ages, the Renaissance, in the Regency, the
Victorian and other eras.

Relive within these books the endless ages of
romance, set against authentic historical
backgrounds. Two new historical love stories
published each month.

HIST-A-1